"The gunma
debris above

Sophie noticed the last two shots had hit close together on the pile. A few bricks and boards were sliding; a few other chunks began to wiggle and fall. She and Bridger had nowhere to go. If they ran out from their shelter, it would give the gunmen an open shot.

But if they stayed...

The sound of slipping picked up in intensity. Sophie's chest seized with fear. They had hesitated for too long. From somewhere in the pile, a child's toy began to play music. It was so eerie it gave Sophie chills.

In a sudden quaking motion, whatever was holding the debris came loose like a dam releasing a flood. Bridger tried to push Sophie aside as the avalanche tumbled down, but she grabbed for Kai, nudging her out of the way.

A chaotic storm of noise, dust and confusion was all Sophie registered before everything went black...

Sommer Smith teaches high school English and adores animals. She loves reading romances and writing about fairy tales. She started writing her first novel when she was thirteen and has wanted to write romances since. Her three children provide her inspiration for her stories with their many antics. With two dogs and a horse to keep her active in between, Sommer stays busy traveling to ball games and colleges in two states.

Books by Sommer Smith

Love Inspired Suspense

Under Suspicion
Attempted Abduction
Ranch Under Siege
Wyoming Cold Case Secrets
Wyoming Ranch Ambush
Deadly Treasure Hunt
Deadly Ranch Abduction
Texas Christmas Pursuit

Visit the Author Profile page at LoveInspired.com.

TEXAS CHRISTMAS PURSUIT

SOMMER SMITH

If you purchased this book without a cover you should be aware that this book is stolen property. It was reported as "unsold and destroyed" to the publisher, and neither the author nor the publisher has received any payment for this "stripped book."

LOVE INSPIRED® SUSPENSE
INSPIRATIONAL ROMANCE

ISBN-13: 978-1-335-95744-3

Recycling programs for this product may not exist in your area.

Texas Christmas Pursuit

Copyright © 2025 by Sommer Smith

All rights reserved. No part of this book may be used or reproduced in any manner whatsoever without written permission.

Without limiting the author's and publisher's exclusive rights, any unauthorized use of this publication to train generative artificial intelligence (AI) technologies is expressly prohibited.

This is a work of fiction. Names, characters, places and incidents are either the product of the author's imagination or are used fictitiously. Any resemblance to actual persons, living or dead, businesses, companies, events or locales is entirely coincidental.

For questions and comments about the quality of this book, please contact us at CustomerService@Harlequin.com.

® is a trademark of Harlequin Enterprises ULC.

Love Inspired
22 Adelaide St. West, 41st Floor
Toronto, Ontario M5H 4E3, Canada
www.LoveInspired.com

Printed in Lithuania

MIX
Paper | Supporting responsible forestry
FSC® C021394

But judgment shall return unto righteousness:
and all the upright in heart shall follow it.
—*Psalm* 94:15

To my daughter Gracie, for you make my heart happy with your kindness, virtue and goodness. Your dedication and perseverance in all you do are an inspiration. Keep smiling, baby girl!

ONE

Sophie Wilder was heartsick at the devastation before her. An entire community on the edge of Garland, Texas, was flattened.

How could wind create such a disaster? She had seen the work of an estimated EF4 tornado on television before, but never firsthand, and while she was from Texas, she lived about two hours away from Garland, outside of Paris, where she had never seen one on quite this large a scale. And usually when this type of storm struck, it was in the spring, not in December, meaning no one had expected it to reach such a magnitude.

It would sure put a damper on the upcoming Christmas season for many folks.

Kai, her Bernese Mountain dog trained in search and rescue, seemed horrified by the destruction as well. The dog plucked her way morosely over the rubble surrounding them. Her long, furry tail drooped lower than usual, and her typical exuberant manner had dropped off somewhere between Sophie's red Jeep Rubicon and the edge of the storm debris.

Sophie had released the clasp holding Kai's leash to her official SAR vest, but instead of bounding off to begin her work, Kai lowered her large, fluffy head and sighed. Was she overwhelmed trying to decide where to begin? Sophie certainly was. This was their first experience with an assignment of such magnitude.

The path of the tornado had covered over a mile in width and almost three in length before ending its tirade through neighborhoods and subdivisions, sucking up everything in its path before spitting it all back onto the stripped-bare landscape. Homes and businesses lay scattered like forgotten matchsticks, bricks and siding alike beaten into mere fragments of what they had once been. But if the weather felt apocalyptic already, it was going to get worse. Meteorologists had predicted that the unusual weather pattern was just getting started and, by some time later this evening, they now expected freezing rain and possible snow flurries. That meant any survivors had to be found today or they risked freezing in the extreme conditions.

"Kai, find." Sophie hoped her voice would convey her eagerness to get to work and influence her canine's attitude as well. She tucked her shoulder-length, sandy-blond hair behind her ears as she watched the dog work.

It wasn't long before Kai began to zigzag back and forth in a gradually narrowing pattern that told Sophie she had picked up on something. Kai was primarily an air-scenting dog, trained to find the smallest traces of human odor on the wind, and even in a circumstance like this one, she could home in on a person because that's what she had been carefully schooled to do. Her nose amazed Sophie.

The temperature was already beginning to drop as Sophie carefully picked her way over to where the large dog had begun to sniff at the debris, and she shivered in her light jacket. Kai's zigzagging course had narrowed to a fine point, leading them there. Sophie didn't see anyone yet. But, if possible, residents had likely sheltered underground and, if not, deep within interior walls of the structures to avoid as much flying debris as imaginable. Sophie saw no signs of a cellar, only what was left of a house.

Sophie didn't know how the residents could have survived this storm. Water pooled in the floors of places that might have once been kitchens and bathrooms, their tiled floorings splintered and buckled in some places while left perfectly intact in others. There were no discernable patterns, just chaos left in the tornado's wake.

So much waste. It was overwhelming to see it firsthand.

Sophie didn't have time to dwell on it long before Kai began to give the telltale signs that she had found something. When Kai alerted, Sophie was there to respond.

However, Kai began to whine, her ears falling back low on her head. Sophie knew her body language well. This wasn't likely a survivor. As good as Kai was at her job, she wanted to find her people alive, and so did Sophie. Truthfully, Sophie and Kai had only worked on one rescue where the missing person had been found deceased, and they had been with a large team of other people at the time.

That wasn't exactly the case today. Many others on the team were here, but the tornado's damage was widespread, so they had each been given their own quadrants to try to find any possible survivors as quickly as necessary before the next round of inclement weather moved in.

"Good girl, Kai. What is it? What have you found, huh?" Sophie presented Kai's toy—her reward for a job well done—but the dog whimpered instead of getting excited. She accepted the toy, but only mouthed it a bit and then stood with her tail drooping.

Something was definitely wrong.

Carefully, Sophie edged forward. A pale, slender hand appeared amid the wreckage as she stepped closer, barely visible amid the scraps of what had once been a house. The debris could have landed there from anywhere, though. The only way Sophie could discern that it had once been a house standing in this spot was that, oddly enough, parts of it were still standing, if not completely intact. The hand itself was small and delicate in appearance, leading Sophie to believe it belonged to a woman or an older child.

Either way, it made her stomach churn.

Sophie kept speaking softly to Kai as she followed protocol. Easing as close as she dared in the shifty rubble, Sophie called out to the victim.

"Hello? Can you hear me? I'm here to help." She spoke clearly and loud enough for her voice to penetrate the mass of discarded bricks and boards.

But there wasn't even the slightest sound or movement in response. Her victim could be unconscious, but in the aftermath of a storm of this magnitude, she doubted that was the case. It was more likely she was indeed dead.

Sophie hoped with all her heart she was wrong. She called in on her walkie-talkie and reported her find, photographing the scene with her phone. She began to carefully remove the boards and Sheetrock piled atop the victim. Chunks of brick, soiled fabrics and bits of miscellaneous debris were mixed in among the timbers, evidence that everything from furniture, curtains, mangled garden planters and broken kitchen appliances had been smashed and scattered in the fierce storm winds. Fragmented glass littered the mess, as well, making Sophie immensely grateful for the work gloves protecting her hands. Nearly choking from the dust stirred up by the splintered drywall, she finally uncovered the most telling portion of the half-buried victim. It was undeniably a female, and she was most definitely not just unconscious.

Sophie jerked back at the realization but took a deep breath to calm herself. She reminded herself this went along with working on a search and rescue team. It wasn't always a happy ending. However, when her thoughts cleared, she realized something was off about this storm victim. The dirt and filth covering everything else couldn't hide the telltale gunshot wound in the woman's head, centered in her forehead as if she had been killed execution-style.

Sophie's gasp came loudly in the quiet morning air, and Kai whimpered again, but the dog didn't move. Sophie's middle clenched tightly as the impact of the situation sank into her more fully, and she wanted to cling to Kai for comfort. Her canine was working, though, and as much as she loved to snuggle her at home, right now she needed to let her work. She swallowed hard as she backed away to wait for assistance.

Sophie's legs shook and her hands were trembling as she dropped the long, flat piece of broken Sheetrock she had just picked up. She stumbled backward. What should she do? Where was her help?

Looking around, she confirmed that no one else from the rescue crews was anywhere in sight. She saw no paramedics or firefighters headed her way. What was taking so long?

She had to find help.

Trembling, she pulled her walkie-talkie from her belt loop again, reminding the coordinator that she had requested help. "I need assistance from the police. It doesn't appear the storm could have had anything to do with the death of this victim. There's a gunshot wound to the victim's head."

The static paused as the coordinator replied. "We'll notify the authorities. There's a check station near you." But that was all Sophie received before the voice faded into static once more.

Frustrated, she accepted the vague response and waited. After a few minutes, she decided to take matters into her own hands. She didn't really want to walk all the way back to the check-in station, but she supposed it was better than staying there alone with a dead body. Especially one that had obviously been murdered.

"Kai, come!" Sophie picked up her backpack and commanded the dog to sit so she could reconnect Kai's leash. Licking her lips as she waited, the canine sat obediently while Sophie fastened the clasp. Then Sophie recorded the GPS coordinates so that she could find the victim again. She grasped Kai's leash and started walking with her toward the check-in station.

It was an eerie feeling being out there practically alone except for Kai, especially after such a devastating storm. She could see people moving around the wreckage at a distance. From their posts, their voices barely carried to her on the wind. The scene was too quiet, even though rescue trucks and emergency vehicles moved about along the outskirts of the area. The morning had dawned sunny and clear, but clouds were creeping in again now, making her surroundings terribly gloomy in the face of the aftermath. Despite the gray sky, Sophie could see for what seemed like dozens of miles across the flat landscape where the homes and businesses that had once risen against the skyline now stretched flat before her. Yet she still felt the pressing gloom of her solitude. She shivered.

Sophie hadn't gone far when she heard the hum of an engine and turned her head to see a large UTV had begun to make its way through the debris, moving her way. She held loosely to Kai's leash and walked toward it. Sophie noticed that the man behind the wheel wore a cowboy hat and sunglasses, along with a dark-colored Carhartt barn jacket. Disappointment filled her. She had hoped someone had sent an officer in her direction, but this man wore plain clothes. Maybe he would at least give her and Kai a ride to the check-in station.

But as the vehicle rolled to a stop beside her a few minutes later, the man produced a badge encased in a wallet before she could speak. "Detective Bridger Cole with the Texas Rangers. Are you the woman who radioed in about a suspicious victim?"

Sophie hesitated. A Texas Ranger? She hadn't expected that. "Uh, yes. I'm Sophie Wilder and this is my SAR dog, Kai. She found the victim."

Nodding, he gave an appreciative glance toward the dog, earning him a few points with Sophie despite his brusque manner. "You're sure about the victim? She wasn't killed in the storm?"

She nodded. "I saw a—a gunshot wound. In her forehead."

Detective Cole pulled off his sunglasses, frowning. Deep turquoise eyes probed her face and she was surprised to see a touch of sympathy there. "I guess that's pretty hard to mistake."

He was even more handsome up close, and the brilliant color of his eyes caused Sophie's pulse to hitch. "I dropped a pin. I can send you the location."

She opened her phone before looking to him for direction on where to send the pin.

He shook his head. "Never mind that. Hop in. You can show me. I have some questions to ask you as well." He made a gesture to the seat beside him before returning the sunglasses to his handsome face. "I assume your dog rides okay?"

Sophie didn't move right away. Did he expect her to put Kai in the back of the UTV? If so, Sophie would ride back there as well. Kai was a large dog, but Sophie wouldn't separate from her. They were a team and it was up to Sophie to ensure Kai's safety. "She rides fine."

"Will she be too crowded on the seat between us?" Detective Cole patted the space and Sophie's shoulders relaxed.

"No. No, she will probably lean on me anyway." Sophie commanded Kai to load up into the UTV. She liked Detective Cole just a little more then, too.

As soon as Sophie climbed in beside Kai, the detective surprised her once more. "Are you okay, Miss Wilder?"

Her head snapped around to him. He was looking at her, one hand on the ignition key, but she couldn't see his eyes behind the sunglasses. His voice held genuine concern, however.

"I... Yeah. No. I'm not really sure yet. I mean I'm supposed to be accustomed to seeing the occasional deceased victim as part of a SAR team, but..." She didn't explain that she and Kai hadn't been FEMA-certified for long and that she had only ever encountered something like this once before while accompanied by another SAR handler and their dog. She already felt a little inadequate as well as rattled.

"But it's different when it's a murder." He'd finished with exactly what she had wanted to say but couldn't choke out. "And the truth is, you never really get used to that, either."

She was about to send him a questioning glance when he made a broad sweeping motion around them to indicate the destruction left behind by the previous night's tornado. Sophie could only nod, so thick was the lump in her throat.

"Disaster relief should be here soon. The local crews have more than they can do at the moment." He clicked on the ignition.

"I know many people will be grateful for that." Sophie gestured in the general direction of where Kai had found the body. "It's that way."

He acknowledged her directive with a nod as he put the UTV in motion. Sophie didn't outright study the man, but she was hyperaware of him sitting just on the other side of Kai. He was large, probably a good bit over six feet, and his frame was solid and lean. He seemed young for a Ranger detective but looks were sometimes deceiving, and she really didn't know much about the qualifications. Honestly, he wasn't what she would have expected to find in a seasoned law enforcement officer in a city as large as Garland, Texas. He brought to mind a larger-than-life character from television or something, with his relaxed manner and cowboy hat and boots.

Sophie pulled her thoughts inward, forcing her concentration to the scene—and victim—before them. Who was she? Why had she been murdered? If it had happened shortly before the storm hit, could her killer still be nearby as well? What if the killer was alive and they pulled him from the rubble without knowing?

She shivered once more at the thought.

Kai whined twice beside her as she sensed Sophie's angst, the dog's huge brown eyes rising from where she rested her head on Sophie's lap. The canine licked at her upper lip, pink tongue flicking out just below the freckles spotting the white fur there beside her nose. Sophie stroked Kai's fur comfortingly, speaking to her in hushed tones.

"Beautiful dog. You don't see a lot of Bernies around here." Detective Cole spoke above the roar of the machine.

Kai wasn't the most common search and rescue dog breed, but she knew her job and strove to please, and she was surprisingly agile despite her size.

"She's a hard worker and my constant companion. Have you ever worked with a Bernese Mountain dog yourself?" Sophie lifted her eyes from Kai to Detective Cole.

He shook his head. "No, I'm only familiar with the breed because a friend of mine owned one growing up. His dog's name was Benson. I stayed over at their house a few times, and his dog was always with us wherever we went as we got older. Pretty sure Benson thought he was human."

He gave a little chuckle at the fond memory and Sophie found it helped her relax just a tiny bit.

"Are you still friends?" She wondered how long ago it had been, but she didn't ask, thinking he should decide how much to share with her. She had very few friends she had kept up with since her youth, but she wondered if it was the same for him.

"Yes, but we don't see each other often. Blake lives in southern Texas now." Detective Cole's tone had grown distant toward the end of his reply, leaving Sophie to follow his gaze out of curiosity. He was watching a shadow in the distance.

"Is there someone there?" Sophie couldn't keep the concern from her tone. Her tension immediately returned. It had been the same zing of awareness racing through her when Kai had alerted on the body. Something wasn't right.

"I'm not sure, but I think so. Are we getting close?" Detective Cole had one hand on his service weapon. A helicopter's blades beat the air at a steady rhythm in the distance. It was getting closer, but it faded into obscurity as Sophie focused on their surroundings.

She had to raise her voice to be heard over the helicopter. "Yes, it's just right—"

A splintering crack against the fiberglass on the side of the UTV interrupted her words.

"Get down! Low as you can." Detective Cole had already drawn his SIG to begin firing back as Sophie tugged Kai as far down beside her on the floor as she could. There wasn't much room in the vehicle, but Kai obediently hunkered into Sophie's small frame, making herself as small as possible. She let out a soft whine as the sharp report of the detective's handgun stung her tender ears.

Sophie spoke soothingly to her despite her own fears. The detective, also hunkered low, fired off a few more rounds.

"Hang on. I'm gonna try to head for some cover." He spoke softly, in complete control. It eased Sophie's anxiety just a bit.

Sophie didn't have any idea where he planned to find cover out in this wide-open disaster area, swept flat by the storm. But she prayed he would get them there soon.

Bridger considered the petite woman he found himself protecting from the corner of his eye as he kept tabs on the shots coming from behind a nearby pile of rubble. She seemed so delicate and out of place amid their dystopian surroundings with her big hazel eyes and innocent demeanor.

Crews with heavy-duty extraction equipment had begun to arrive and the few dozen people wandering around for more than a mile in every direction seemed completely unaware of their distress, thanks to the racket of the helicopter overhead. It was probably just a news crew looking for an emotional aerial shot of the wreckage to air on the next segment. The shooter had been smart enough to wait for the opportunity to mask the noise of the gunshots.

As Bridger sped away as fast as he safely could with his passengers, he had to weave to avoid debris littering the ground all around them. The woman clutched her dog as they swerved and bounced, and Bridger wasn't sure if it was for safety or comfort. *Probably both.*

A shot narrowly missed a tire as the shooter tried another tactic. Bridger raised his SIG and fired back. A spray of dust and debris kicked up in the wake of the bullet.

The helicopter above them began to drift away, and as the gunman realized it, he dropped his weapon and fled. A figure in all gray clothing dashed from the mass of bricks, and Bridger turned to follow. He didn't make it far in the UTV, however, so he brought the off-road vehicle to a stop and hopped out.

"Stay here and stay low." He called the words over his right shoulder as he climbed from the seat.

The shooter had gained a good head start while Bridger parked the UTV, so he had to push hard to scramble over the debris and keep the man in sight. The gray-clad man ducked behind every bit of brick and mortar he could find still standing and it wasn't long before Bridger lost sight of him completely. He suspected the man had found a hiding place, but he was too far from the UTV and the woman the gunman had been targeting to search for long.

Unless his gut was wrong—and it usually wasn't—Sophie Wilder had just unintentionally landed herself in a great deal of danger.

Giving up the search, he sprinted back to the UTV. She watched him warily, her arms still thrown protectively over her beautiful dog, who squirmed just a bit in excitement at his return, tail thumping hard against the seat.

"He's gone?" Sophie's expression was a mixture of relief and disappointment. She clearly knew Bridger hadn't caught the man, but at least there would be no more gunshots for now. He understood her mixed feelings—he would much rather have taken the shooter in to get some answers.

"He is. Let's get a look at the scene before he decides to come back and try again." He rubbed a dingy spot from the lens of his sunglasses with the edge of his shirt and put them back on.

She climbed out of the UTV and commanded her dog to follow. "It's just right over here."

It was no wonder the man had tried to lead them away when his shooting hadn't scared them off. He had probably watched Sophie leave in search of help.

It took a moment to navigate the mounds of destruction, but once they reached the victim, Bridger couldn't deny what Sophie had said. The gunshot wound in the forehead stuck out harshly against the pale skin and dirt smudges on the woman's face. The storm had done nothing to help the killer hide his victim. Part of the room where the body lay had been spared from the storm, over half of a wall still standing despite the mess just a few feet off where the perpendicular wall was completely gone. None of the destruction made sense. It was as if the storm had been a living, breathing thing with a conscience, and had wanted no part of covering up this man's crimes.

"I did pull those two pieces of broken Sheetrock aside, but I didn't disturb the scene otherwise. I saw a hand sticking out, and I didn't know if the victim was living or dead." She explained her actions in a rapid tone, as if afraid she would be reprimanded for disturbing the scene.

"You didn't do anything wrong." He narrowed his eyes as he stepped closer, observing the area around the victim. Where the part of one wall still stood, a pantry door hung wretchedly from its hinges at an odd angle. Next to it, splintered glass shards from a window littered the floor and the gnarled remainder of a light fixture lay twisted against a broken microwave. There was some sort of damp residue on the remaining floor tiles, which were broken in several places but not missing from the foundation. His guess was that a kitchen had once occupied the room, for several junction boxes were visible near the remaining walls and on the floor, as if heavy appliances had been wired into the space. He couldn't tell if the liquid was rainwater or something else, but he made a mental note to have it checked out.

Just a few yards away, in what was likely the living room, nothing remained except a slab of concrete and a random board or brick here and there that had been swept in by the twister.

Bridger had lived in Texas for most of his life, and while the majority of the numerous tornadoes that struck the state resulted in minimal damage and loss of life, a devastating storm like this one came along just often enough to remind citizens of how deadly they could be. It was humbling, to be sure.

Returning his concentration to the victim, he snapped a couple of photos to record the scene then called it in, requesting a full forensic workup. Maybe the storm had hit before the killer could get rid of any evidence he might have left behind.

Bridger had almost forgotten Sophie's presence until she spoke quietly from behind him.

"Are Kai and I free to go now?" She was looking away

from the scene when he turned, her expression pained, and he realized just how traumatic this all must be for her.

"I'd like to speak to you a little more about exactly how you found the scene first. And after that episode with the shooter, I think you might need a little protection until we catch the killer." He kept his tone even and gentle, hoping it might help with the news.

It didn't.

She turned pale. "You don't really think the killer will come after me, do you? Just because I found the body? Surely, he was just trying to scare us away."

He wished he could spare her further exposure to this but he couldn't. He needed her help. And she seemed to have no idea how much she needed protection. When it sank in that someone had just been shooting at her with no concern for her life, she might rethink wanting to just up and leave.

He spared a glance at her dog. "It might not only be that. Typically, someone who kills their victim execution-style like this is an experienced criminal. He's probably wanted for more than just a murder. And if he's killed before, he won't think twice about doing it again to keep his crimes and identity hidden."

"He doesn't think we can track him, does he? Kai doesn't have anything to go on in order to hunt him down. Unless something is found at the scene with his scent, she wouldn't be able to find him." Her voice had taken on an edge.

"He might not realize that. There's also a chance that he believes you saw him and can identify him. He's been lurking about, presumably to see if his crime was discovered." Bridger made a sweeping motion with one arm. "It's clear you've just become a target."

"So…you think he would be willing to kill me, too, just

to keep me silent? I'm in that much danger?" Sophie's arms came up and wrapped around her upper body.

"I think—" he paused and looked around them as a fire rescue truck appeared a few yards away, headed in their direction "—we are *both* in danger until he's caught."

TWO

"My director has suggested I keep you close to ensure your protection." Bridger had ended the call just before breaking the news to Sophie. The way he'd emphasized *suggested* told her it was likely more of an order. To his credit, however, his expression remained neutral.

"I see. And what, exactly, does that mean?" Sophie studied Kai's soft fur shining in the bright daylight. A few firefighters and officers were buzzing around the area now, as well, but Sophie was ready to get away from the scene.

Bridger shifted his stance. "I think it best if you stay with me until we sort this whole thing out. I live on a ranch about a half-hour's drive from here."

Her attention returned to his face. "Detective Cole, I—"

"Might as well call me Bridger. Where do you live?" He didn't let her continue with the argument she was trying to voice.

"I live between Bonham and Paris, but my mother lives with me. My father passed away when I was young and she's now divorced from my stepfather. I don't want to put her in any danger. Do you think this guy would follow me out of town?" Sophie was referring to the man who had just been shooting at them. She couldn't keep the frown from her face. The situation put her in a difficult position.

His sunglasses hid his expression, but his voice was kind. "I'm sorry to hear about your father. But I'd like you to at least consider staying with me. That's a pretty long commute if we need to question you further. Not to mention, it could put your mother in danger, as well, if you return home before he's apprehended. I can have someone keep an eye on your place on the off chance that this guy manages to figure out who you are and trace you back to your residence, but I think it would be best if you stay in the area until we figure this out."

"Am I being asked not to leave town? Like, officially?" Sophie felt her heartbeat begin to quicken. Heat suffused her face. Did she watch too much television?

"Not like that." He gave her a reassuring grin. "You aren't a suspect."

"I don't know much about how this works. Do you live alone?" Sophie suddenly realized she knew nothing about this man. Did he have a wife and children at home? Roommates? He had mentioned a ranch. Did he live with his parents?

"My mother, sister and two younger brothers also live there and work on the ranch. You'll be well protected there." He paused. "And we're all trustworthy. My brothers are good guys. And I think you'll like my mom and sister."

Sophie still hesitated. "I'd hate to put anyone else in danger, though."

"I think my brothers and I can handle it." He grinned "They also both work in law enforcement. We have good security, as well, and my mom and my sister both know how to handle a gun."

Sophie nodded. That was more than she knew. "I guess I don't have much choice. I can't handle this thing on my own."

"I'd rather you didn't try. Besides, I could use your help with a few things concerning the case." He turned away. "Right now, I need to get the scene taped off before it's contaminated. It will only take a few minutes, and then we can get you out of here."

He strode over to the UTV and retrieved a black duffel bag. Sophie watched him work while Kai settled at her side with a slight grunt. The dog seemed just as troubled by the events of their day as Sophie was, so she was glad to give her a little time to rest.

Bridger finished up the necessary processing of the scene while Sophie checked in with the incident commander in charge of rescue efforts via text message. The news that he had excused Sophie and Kai for the remainder of the day didn't seem to come as a surprise to Bridger. In fact, he asked if she would accompany him to one of the local police precincts where he might access a secure connection to complete his files on the case and access missing persons. He wanted her help with trying to identify the victim. She reluctantly agreed.

"I'd prefer to transport Kai in my own vehicle, if that's possible. I'd like to be able to secure her, and my Jeep is equipped properly to do so." Sophie stroked the dog behind her ears, Kai's soulful brown eyes gazing up at her adoringly.

"I can just ride with you, if that makes it easier." Bridger gestured toward the UTV. "I need to take care of the UTV before we go, though."

She nodded. "I'm parked at the east check-in station. Where do you need to take it?"

"My truck and trailer are close to there as well. Hop in and we'll head that way." He tossed his bag into the back.

By the time they had secured the UTV to the trailer and

made it to the station, Sophie's expression was weighted with the marks of defeat.

"Are you okay?" Bridger kept his voice low as he held open the door to an empty office inside the building. A captain had assured him they wouldn't be disturbed there.

"I'm fine. Just feeling a bit overwhelmed by all of this." Sophie guided Kai into the room and clicked off her leash, allowing the dog to relax in a corner.

"This shouldn't take long." He couldn't shake the feeling that the woman Sophie had found was somehow familiar. An officer offered them both coffee and Sophie accepted with a grateful smile. Bridger took a Styrofoam cup, as well, but settled it beside him on the desk while she sipped hers.

He filtered through photos he had collected related to the case, but nothing was a hit. They had similar results with missing persons. Sophie, who had been peering at the screen behind him, stepped back and shook her head.

"She's not there." She sighed.

He had clicked to the end of the files. Sophie was right. If the woman was related to the case he had been working on when he arrived, there was no record of her. And she hadn't been reported missing. That meant she was either not involved at all, under the radar up until this point, or she was someone who'd gotten in the way of the criminals plaguing the drug scene in the area.

He spoke the question pestering him aloud. "What are we missing?"

He was sitting back in his chair, pondering the situation, when an email notification appeared in the top right-hand side of his screen. It was marked urgent, so he clicked to bring it up. It was from the FBI.

He hadn't realized Sophie had stepped close once more,

but she drew in a sharp breath when a thumbnail photo of a woman in a suit popped up. "That's her. What is this about?"

"Missing person alert. The woman is a DEA agent who's been working undercover. She hasn't reported to her supervisor in over twenty-four hours and they haven't been able to contact her." Bridger scanned the message and relayed the information to Sophie. "They request anyone with information about her notify the FBI immediately."

Sophie sucked in another breath. "Looks like her cover was blown."

Sophie paced back and forth across the tiny office, Kai watching her with her head on her paws. Her fear ratcheted up a notch. If the woman was undercover DEA and had been found out, what did that tell her about the man who had been shooting at them?

This was bad news. Very bad news indeed.

He was not only a killer but likely also a hardened criminal who would stop at nothing to maintain his freedom and anonymity, just as Bridger had said. Even going so far as to murder a federal agent.

She had hoped he was wrong about her becoming a target.

Detective Cole was on the phone, reporting their discovery, but Sophie couldn't focus on what he was saying. Her imagination kept distracting her with new concerns over this latest revelation.

When he finished the call, he turned to her with a harrowing expression. "You might want to sit down."

Sophie resisted the urge to cover her eyes with her hand. She had known when she'd trained in search and rescue that there might be some danger involved. But this went beyond any of her previous imaginings.

"Just tell me." She hovered next to the chair, though, just in case.

"The DEA officer, Sasha Benton, was undercover, trying to pinpoint the leader of a local drug trafficking organization that's reportedly responsible for supplying a variety of illegal drugs—many of which have recently been laced with fentanyl—to other crime syndicates all over the country. This is an enormous operation, one that's caused numerous deaths, particularly among teens and college students. Agent Benton went missing shortly before the storm hit and the last thing she told her superiors was that she had names and photos, but she had to get to a secure location to send them. She was planning to report back this morning." He paused. "The problem is, the FBI doesn't want to compromise the entire operation just yet. They want to try to keep her death and true identity a secret for the time being."

"Wow." Sophie didn't know what else to say. She finally sat down, mouth agape.

"You're in a lot of danger right now, Sophie. These people are ruthless. If they think you know anything at all, they won't stop looking for you until you're out of the way. Unless we can ferret them out first. Did you see anything at all besides the body when you first got to the scene? Personal belongings, a handbag, wallet, containers of any sort, anything that could have been used as a weapon? The guy was hanging around, so he could have retrieved any condemning evidence before you led me back to the body. If he'd known she had pictures, he most likely would have taken her phone." Detective Cole seemed to be speaking his thoughts aloud as much as talking to her.

"Nothing I can think of. There was so much debris,

though. It would be hard for anything to stand out much in that mess. I'm not really sure *what* I saw, honestly." Sophie looked over at Kai.

"Well, we may be called upon to search it out. If her cover was blown, there might be a trail. We need to find any personal devices of hers that might still be around, maybe a laptop. If she knew they were on to her, she probably stashed it somewhere, maybe a backup on a flash drive or something." Bridger walked across the room as he explained.

"Shouldn't this be FBI jurisdiction now? I'm not sure Kai and I will be much help finding electronic devices." Sophie had to be honest. She was terrified over becoming involved in this, but she was afraid she had landed herself right in the middle of it. She didn't seem to have a choice.

"It is, but like I said, they want it to look like they are keeping their distance until any remaining evidence can be discovered. There's a small chance the leaders of the drug ring didn't know who she was working for yet." Bridger put both hands on his hips. "But that means we need to act quickly as well."

Sophie was shaking her head. "How did this happen? I just wanted to help storm victims."

His expression changed, softening. "I get that. But it's going to be a while before we can be sure you're safe."

She inhaled deeply, squaring her shoulders. As much as she would like to run from it, she knew what the right thing would be to do. "A woman is dead because of these people. I'm terrified, but if I can help track down her killer, I will. I'm already in danger if what you say is correct. So, where do we start?"

Unexpected pride in her bravery swelled up within Bridger. He forced the feelings away. He couldn't afford to get involved—not with Sophie or any other woman. The women who got too close to him had a way of meeting an unhappy end and he wouldn't have that happen to her.

He reined in his thoughts, realizing Sophie still waited for his reply. "We need to backtrack Agent Benton's steps. If we can learn where she was staying before she was killed, maybe we can find her devices. Until then, her FBI colleagues are going to work on hacking into her accounts to see if she saved anything to the cloud that might help."

Sophie nodded. "Is there a way to figure out how she got here? There was a sedan near the rubble where she was discovered. Could it be her transportation?"

Bridger felt a small twinge of hopefulness. "Possibly. Probably not her vehicle, but we can check for any DNA or prints. Can you describe the vehicle?"

Sophie grimaced. "From what I could tell after the storm damage, I believe it was a deep red color, like a garnet or whatever they call it now. I can't be positive, but I think maybe a late-model Chevy Malibu. The windows were tinted. Four doors. Just a fairly basic sedan. A tree was laying across the hood."

"Excellent. I'll get someone on it." He placed a quick call, hoping she was right.

When he disconnected, he motioned for Sophie and Kai to rise. "Let's get going."

It didn't take them long to load Kai and get moving once the dispatchers and officers in the station had given Kai a little attention and admiration. Sophie patiently answered all the questions about the Bernese Mountain dog while Kai enjoyed some scratching behind the ears before the trio found themselves alone in Sophie's vehicle once again.

"I'll need to stop for fuel before we head out of town. There's a pretty good drive to get to my ranch. We'll head back to retrieve my truck, and then I want you to follow closely the whole way so I can see you in my mirrors. I'd have you go in front of me, but it's easier than trying to direct you, and GPS is a bit confusing in some spots. I'll keep you on the phone while we drive, if that helps." Bridger had an uneasy feeling, but he couldn't really think of a better way. He couldn't just leave his truck indefinitely, and Sophie would want Kai in the vehicle equipped for the dog's safety. Having a friend or family member get the truck and UTV would take far too long. He and Sophie would just have to be extra careful.

Sophie glanced back at Kai, where she sat panting happily. "Fine. I'll fuel up, as well, while we are at the station. I'm a good driver. As long as you don't speed off and leave me, we should be okay."

He chuckled. "I promise to drive at a reasonable speed and, if it looks like I'm losing you, I'll ease off. But we'll need to go the full speed limit. I don't want to waste any time getting you out of town."

She shuddered as his meaning soaked in. "Maybe the shooter from the scene is gone. There are surely too many law enforcement officers around the storm area for him to want to stick around." Sophie bit her lip. Her tone was hopeful but it wavered.

He could tell she didn't really believe this was over any more than he did.

Sophie was trying to hold it together. As the reality of what was happening lodged itself into her brain, fear flared within her as well. Her protector wore a fierce expression as he pulled her Jeep into the designated parking area where he had left his truck. It looked exactly as he had left it, so she was a bit surprised by his words when he spoke. She had really just wanted to come out and volunteer and make it back home to be with her mother by Christmas.

It was starting to look like that might not happen.

Bridger remained unaware of the direction of her thoughts. "Go ahead and get in the driver's seat but pay attention. If I see anything suspicious anywhere on my rig, I need you to be ready to get out of here and quickly."

"Suspicious?" she echoed. "Like what?"

"If the perp saw us bring the UTV here earlier, he could have waited until we were out of sight and planted an explosive device. Until we know his MO, we need to take precautions." Bridger's voice remained even despite the cold it sent flooding through Sophie's body.

"A bomb?" She felt her face drain.

He simply nodded and pushed the door open.

"Oh, I see." She squeezed the words through her tight throat.

He eyed her for a moment. "You all right?"

This time it was her turn to nod. She swallowed hard. "Fine."

He laid a hand over hers, leaving warmth to flood her from there all the way through her toes. She felt her eyes widen as they met his. "Hey, Sophie, I know this is a lot to process right now. But I need you to keep a clear head until we can get you somewhere safe. Then we can concentrate on solving the murder. Can you focus for me? Kai and I are counting on you."

"Right." She took a deep breath. "I'm okay."

When he was sure that she was, Bridger stepped out of the SUV and began going over his vehicle, followed by the trailer and the UTV. He turned and gave her a thumbs-up before climbing into the cab of his truck.

As he pulled away from the parking area, she trailed him to a busy gas station a couple of miles away. When they pulled into the pumps, however, a white sedan followed them and then crept by slowly. The windows were darkly tinted, so Sophie tried to get a tag number, but all she could see was a paper dealer tag. She couldn't read anything more.

When she got out to pump gas, she realized Bridger had noticed the suspicious car as well. He watched it while keeping Sophie in full view.

"Get back into your Jeep. I'm going to pump your fuel. Try to stay out of sight." He waved away the debit card she tried to give him.

Sophie got back in her Rubicon and waited, eyes restlessly scanning the busy area and the streets around them, but the white sedan seemed to have disappeared. Kai whined a couple of times, sensing her anxiety.

"I know, girl. We'll be going soon." Sophie breathed deeply. *In. Out. In. Out. Slow breaths.*

When Bridger tapped on the window, she jumped, letting out a little squeak.

He suppressed a small grin. "Time to go."

Glancing around one more time, she let out the air still in her lungs in relief. Nothing else suspicious.

Bridger waited to pull out until it was clear for them both to merge into traffic, but there was a man walking along the sidewalk along the road near the exit. He wore a ball cap that was pulled low over his eyes. He walked with his hands in his pockets and his head ducked down, as if discouraged and on hard times. He stopped as he got close to the spot where she was about to pull out, as if waiting for her to pass.

Just as she began to go, the man jumped in front of her, causing her to yank the wheel to one side as she braked again. He glanced off her driver's-side fender as she stopped the Jeep again. Kai barked. The man jumped up, yelling, and Sophie froze.

Cracking the window, she spoke. "I'm sorry. Are you okay? I thought—"

Before she could finish, he pulled a 9mm and pointed it at her through the glass, barely letting it protrude from his oversized sleeve. "Get out of the car, lady."

She realized her mistake, as she took in the sunglasses under the ball cap just outside her window.

Looking around, she couldn't see Bridger anywhere. His truck and trailer had disappeared into the heavy traffic and she had no idea if he had seen the man jump in front of her before he'd lost sight of her. She prayed he would quickly realize she wasn't behind him.

Kai growled low in the back of the Jeep and the man's gun hand wavered slightly as if he hadn't known the dog was with her.

"Out of the car! Now!" His deep voice resonated with anger, his eyes darting back and forth between her and the back seat.

Sophie put the Jeep in Park and put her hands in the air above the steering wheel. Her heart hammered against her rib cage and her pulse thundered in her ears. "Okay. I'm going to reach for the door handle."

"Nice and slow, now. Is that dog loose?" He gestured slightly with the nose of the gun, hearing the low growl coming from the back seat. His hand still quivered slightly, and she got the feeling he was afraid of dogs.

She shook her head, unsure if that was good or bad news for her. At least Kai wouldn't be injured trying to save her. "No. She's secured."

Kai scratched at her travel crate, deep barks punctuating the growls now. She clearly wanted to put herself between Sophie and the gunman.

Her phone began to ring over the Bluetooth system, but Sophie didn't dare answer. It was Bridger. Hopefully, he would know something was wrong when she didn't pick up.

"Shut it up!" He gestured toward Kai and she knew for sure from his demeanor the man wasn't fond of dogs.

"Kai, cease. Shh, it's okay, girl." Sophie spoke as calmly to Kai as she could, but the canine wasn't fooled. She was acutely aware of what Sophie was feeling. To her credit, though, she obeyed.

Sophie's hand shook violently against the handle of the driver's-side door, and as she eased it open, Kai let out another sharp bark. Her attacker jumped in reaction and Sophie took advantage of his distraction.

She jerked the car door back just enough to gain some momentum before using both hands and one foot to shove it forcefully into the gunman. Caught off guard, he dropped the gun, which went off as it clattered onto the street. People at the station behind them began to scream and shout at the sound of gunshots. Someone yelled to call 9-1-1.

Sophie slammed her door shut as she put the Jeep in Drive and punched the gas. Traffic swerved and brakes squealed as she shot out of the station's entrance. She caught a glimpse of her attacker stumbling out of the way as she peeled off into the line of cars breezing down the street.

What now? How would she find Bridger?

In answer to her question, her phone began to ring again, and she answered this time.

"That was a gutsy move with the attacker, but you almost got yourself killed in traffic." Bridger sounded mildly amused.

"You saw that? I thought I'd lost you." She could barely control her breaths, still coming fast from the adrenaline.

"I saw him a second too late. When I realized what he

was doing, I circled back. I'm behind you now." He waved to her when she looked in the rearview mirror.

"I was afraid you wouldn't make it to me in time." Her voice still quivered.

"You did well for yourself and you're safe for the moment. I called 9-1-1, as well, and officers were pulling in as I pulled out behind you. I'll pass you, if you'll give me some room. We're going to drive in some circles for a bit to make sure we aren't being followed. There could be more than one." He paused. "Just stay on the line with me. We'll disconnect when I feel it's safe to do so."

Shaken as she was at the moment, Sophie kind of hoped he would just stay on the line indefinitely. Strange how reassuring the sound of his voice was, especially considering she had just met him.

He pulled around as soon as she was able to give him room to do so, and Sophie followed him as he took turn after turn. She was about to relax once more when a flash of white flared across her rearview mirror in the distance.

She drew in a deep breath before looking again. She wasn't mistaken, however. The white sedan was gaining ground on them.

Bridger was still on the line, though he had gone mostly quiet, so she only spoke his name softly to get his attention.

"What's wrong?" He must have picked up on her tone.

"Our creepy white car is back. And he's getting closer by the second."

Before he could reply, the sedan sped ahead, the echo of gunshots announcing the intent of the driver.

The crack of a bullet ricocheted off her back windshield glass.

Sophie screamed.

THREE

Sophie's terror echoed over Bridger's Bluetooth speakers as the bullets struck her SUV. Kai barked sharply from her crate. Glancing around his familiar surroundings, he made a quick decision. She was in the outside lane, and though traffic was pretty light, he might be able to manage to cut the guy off.

"Sophie, I'm going to change lanes, but I want you to stay on the outside. When I brake, keep going. I'm going to try to discourage this guy." Bridger took advantage of the gap in traffic while he was still speaking.

"Okay." She accelerated, coming up beside him. "What now?"

The driver of the car fired a couple more shots and she shrieked again. Kai was barking again as well.

"Get on the other line and call the police. I'll stay on this line. And keep driving." Bridger waited until the sedan was flush with his truck then, gritting his teeth, he jerked the wheel, throwing the car off into a drainage ditch beside a convenience store entrance.

The driver had to slowly drive out of the culvert after ramping and bouncing into the cavernous hole, and Bridger merged to position himself behind Sophie as the vehicle that had been behind the white sedan braked to avoid it. Sophie switched back to his line after a minute or two.

"Take this on-ramp to get on the highway, and then wait until I tell you to go anywhere else." Bridger gave Sophie the instructions as the interstate sign came into view.

She did as he directed, but he could see the sedan picking up speed behind him once more.

"Get to the inside lane and I'll follow. Go as fast as you can and we'll try to lose him in traffic. If we get pulled over, at least we'll have some backup." He gave a dry chuckle.

"I'm going. Throttle down." Sophie didn't sound excited about the opportunity to race along the interstate.

"Come on. It'll be fun. Where's your sense of adventure?" He was only partly teasing. "I thought everyone had dreamed of tearing down an open stretch of highway unhindered by speed limits."

"Not in traffic when my adrenaline is already being tested." She sounded like her jaw was clenched tight. He heard Kai whining her agreement in the background.

But Sophie was right. It was nerve-wracking, especially trying to keep his trailer from walking all over the road at higher speeds. He stayed on the line with Sophie for a while, speaking occasional encouraging words, but it didn't take long before the white sedan was back on their tail. It was time to lose this guy.

The trailer behind him hauling the UTV complicated things significantly, but he had to get it home, so they would have to figure something out.

"Bridger? What do we do? Shouldn't the police have reached us by now?" Sophie was slowing down for another vehicle ahead.

He gripped the wheel, in total agreement with her. "They

should. Hang tight. I'm doing my best." He uttered a silent prayer, anxious for help.

At that moment, lights and sirens appeared, sending the white sedan speeding off an exit to try to avoid them. Bridger gave a sigh of relief as he slowed the rig at last, allowing Sophie to do the same.

"The good news is, we're almost to our exit, also. The bad news is that it gets sticky from there." His family ranch was off the beaten path, to put it mildly. They would have to take a couple of two-lane highways across the prairie and then down a pig trail or two.

But the place was beautiful and well worth the trouble it took to get there. He loved their family land more than he could explain.

"I live in a small town. It's no big deal." Sophie chuckled.

He bit his jaw in amusement. "Oh, the town isn't the problem. It's the lack thereof. The closest town is about twenty minutes away."

She laughed and he had to tell the butterflies in his stomach to calm down. Where had that unexpected emotion come from? He shoved it down deep into his gut. He had already experienced his love of a lifetime. In just three short years, before they could marry and start a family, Jamie had been taken away from him. And he wouldn't put another woman in that kind of danger ever again.

Her sweet smile, her bright blue eyes, all the tender feelings he had felt for Jamie, came rushing back, followed by a swarm of regret and loss. It still hurt so much all these years later. He couldn't go through that again.

So, even though he was taking this woman under his protection until they could figure this whole thing out, Sophie would have to remain at arm's distance. He couldn't be more to her than a protector. He wouldn't.

They disconnected and as they drove on in silence, he repeated it to himself like a mantra. He didn't deserve a second chance. And she deserved far better than someone as broken as Bridger.

Sophie noticed a change in Bridger's demeanor as the danger faded away. Was it just the ebbing of adrenaline that had brought out the brooding side of him? She tried not to ponder it too much. She was already becoming far too interested in the man. This was a temporary arrangement, and any kind of interest was something she couldn't afford to indulge in these days.

Still, something about Bridger reminded her of Troy.

Her husband had been solid and dependable in every way. There weren't many men like that left in the world, and she missed him every single day. It was Troy who had encouraged her to get Kai and follow her dream of helping SAR teams. He had been military—army ranger to be exact—before they'd met, and though an injury during a training incident had led him to retire from the military early, he'd still had a passion for helping people and defending the weak.

Right up until a stage four colon cancer diagnosis had stolen their future right out from under them, even at his young age of thirty-two.

Sophie had been devastated. Even though she was five years his junior, she had vowed then and there never to remarry, though Troy had begged her to reconsider. That had been four years ago now.

She was still determined never to let love back into her life.

When she followed Bridger off the exit and then onto a two-lane road that led into nowhere Texas, her thoughts eased. She began to feel more at home in the rural surroundings. She had spent plenty of time in the city in her life—Austin, Dallas, San Antonio and Houston—but she'd been born and raised in the country. It was where she felt the most at peace, despite the unpleasant curves life had thrown at her.

But after following a long dirt road onto another dirt road that was little more than a rutted path, she was shocked to see a sprawling ranch house coming into view. Surely, this wasn't their destination, was it? It was something she might have dreamed up from spending too many hours scrolling through dream homes on Pinterest or watching hours of HGTV.

There weren't many places like it where she was from. If there were any close enough, they'd been surrounded by iron fencing, security systems and locked gates.

But Bridger pulled down the winding dirt lane all the way to the gorgeous white farmhouse, two stories of sparkling windows winking at her in the fading afternoon light, a wraparound porch on the lower level. Christmas wreaths adorned the windows and greenery swept along the railings of the massive porch. Two shiny bay horses grazed just beyond a white split-rail fence and not one but two sprawling red barns stood sentry on either side of and just beyond house. It made her suck in a breath of shock. In the distance, she could see what she thought were Black Angus cattle grazing the still-somehow lush green fields of Bermuda grass.

If she hadn't found a dead body in the rubble just hours ago, she would have thought she was still lounging in her bed asleep.

Rolling down the window, Bridger gestured for her to pull up close to the house. "I'm going to park the trailer around the back by the barn. Go ahead and park and I'll be right here."

Sophie let Kai out to run, still standing beside her Jeep, staring at the house in awe when Bridger returned.

At the same time, a slightly graying woman opened the front door and walked outside.

"Bridger, you brought company?" She squinted as she raised one hand to cover her eyes. The sun always seemed so much more intense after a storm, and Sophie found her own brow furrowed in the bright light. But the other side of the horizon was darkening rapidly with clouds, making the sky look eerie and otherworldly. The wind gusted in that moment, colder than before and reminding them that change was on the way.

"Mom, this is Sophie and her search and rescue dog, Kai. Long story short, they're helping with a case and under my protection." Bridger made a vague gesture toward the pair.

"Oh. Well, it's nice to meet you, Sophie. And you, too, Kai. Please come in. We are about to have some sweet tea and a snack. Dinner will be ready in a couple of hours." She nodded at Sophie as she spoke, her expression kind, and Sophie got the feeling this was nothing new to her.

"It's nice to meet you, too. Uh—Mrs. Cole." She realized Bridger had only referred to her as his mom.

"Just call me Dana." She stepped back and made a motion for Sophie to go ahead of her. "Come on inside. Bring Kai along. I'll get you some tea and a fresh bowl of water for her, too."

Sophie had never felt more readily welcomed by a total stranger in all her life. She followed Bridger's mother to a windowed alcove just off the beautiful sparkling kitchen. Everything was bright and cheerful, covered with Christmas garland and red glitter, and Sophie found the burdens of the day lightening as Dana Cole poured her a tall glass of brilliant amber liquid, ice cubes clacking together as she brought it to the table. Instrumental Christmas music played softly from somewhere in the background and Sophie hummed along to herself.

Kai slurped happily at the large metal bowl full of cool water Mrs. Cole provided and, in a few seconds, was joined by a pair of corgis sniffing at her heels.

"Don't mind these two troublemakers. They think they're descended from the late queen's corgis. This is Diamond and this is Davis." She pointed to the slimmer of the two fluff balls first.

"Oh, hello." Sophie held out a hand for them each to sniff and was dismissed as a nonthreat very decidedly before they began to focus on Kai once more, their furry bottoms wiggling adorably as they walked away.

"Sophie's going to be staying with us for a little while, Mom. I'm going to put her next to Carly's room." Bridger made himself a glass of sweet tea, as well, and stood by a long kitchen bar that ran across the dividing space between the two rooms. He looked large and a little intimidating in the space, she realized.

"That's fine, Bridger. You know our home is always open to whatever you need. May I ask what she's helping you with?" Dana tossed him an overly innocent grin, as if they had played this game before.

"You know I can't talk to you about an open case, Mom. But nice try." He frowned in her direction.

A slightly annoyed voice came from the stairs just then and Sophie turned to see a young woman, maybe early twenties if she were guessing, taking them two at a time. "Bridger, I'm supposed to be having friends over tonight.

A little get-together before Stephanie gets married since we can't all go to Nashville."

The young woman was glaring daggers at Bridger and Sophie could only assume he was the reason she wasn't going.

"That's fine, sis. We won't get in your way. Just don't make too much noise. Some of us have to get up and get to work early." He turned away, grabbing a cookie from a jar near the tea pitcher.

"Sophie, this is Bridger's sister, Carly." Dana Cole made the introduction.

"It's Caroline. I can't convince them I'm not a little girl anymore." She rolled her eyes but stuck out her slender hand in a friendly gesture. "Whoa, is that your dog? How beautiful!"

"This is Kai. She's a trained search and rescue canine," Sophie said. "And it's nice to meet you, Caroline."

Her use of the full name earned her a dazzling smile of appreciation. "Can I pet her?"

"Of course." Sophie smiled back. Bridger's sister was tall and willowy, and if Sophie didn't miss her guess, she could be a real spitfire.

Bridger cleared his throat. "When you've finished your tea, Sophie, if you don't mind, I'd like to go over some things. On the porch. Alone." He shot a look at both his mother and sister, who rolled her eyes.

"Of course. I'm ready whenever." Sophie stood.

Kai followed them onto the back porch and settled herself beside Sophie with a grunt. The wind howled and Sophie found herself wishing she had worn warmer clothing as it cut through her thin athletic wear. But when she turned to face Bridger, she knew the rapidly cooling air was the least of her concerns.

"Sophie, I got a text from a friend of mine, Jackson, at the crime lab. They can't get anyone out to collect what they need from the crime scene because of all the disaster relief efforts going on. It's on me to collect what evidence I can before the ice storm makes it impossible to do so. The longer we wait, the less chance we have of finding anything." Bridger looked pained as he explained it to her.

"You're leaving me here? And your family? Unprotected?" She hated the cracking of her voice. She didn't want to appear afraid. Even though she was.

"No. I'm afraid I need to take you with me. Being first to discover the crime, I can find what I need faster if you accompany me, and time is of the essence. Can you do that?" He glanced back over his shoulder. "We can leave Kai here. She'll be in good hands with my family."

Sophie hesitated. "I hate to leave her."

"We'll get what we need and get back here as quickly as possible. I promise it won't be long." Bridger's tone was firm, though, and she knew she didn't have much choice in the matter.

But a shiver of foreboding accompanied the nod she gave him. Something told her things weren't going to be quite as simple as he made it sound.

FOUR

Bridger had hated to ask Sophie to leave Kai behind when she could prove to be useful on the hunt for evidence, and Sophie had looked a little forlorn having to leave her with his family, but they'd needed to make this trip quickly. The clouds were building rapidly and the temperature had dropped more than ten degrees in the last hour.

He pushed his truck to go as fast as he could carefully manage, thinking they might be able return safely to the ranch before any icy weather hit. With any luck, the ground would be too warm for anything to stick right away. The odds of finding any evidence at the scene were scarce now anyway, thanks to the wind and rain from the storm, not to mention the killer prowling around.

Sophie rode beside him in total silence, watching out the window with an anxious expression for most of the way. A few short miles from the storm site, however, Bridger noticed a dark-colored van with tinted windows approaching rapidly from behind, dodging in and out of traffic with reckless maneuvers. Bridger pressed his lips together and accelerated.

"I think we've attracted company." He glanced at Sophie, whose eyes widened.

"How?" She turned to see the van weaving ever closer.

"I'd say our perp sent out word to watch for my truck and your Jeep, especially around the crime scene." Bridger swerved in behind a fast-moving sedan in the lane to his left, hoping the car coming up behind him now would effectively cut off the van.

But the sedan's driver chose to be courteous, moving into the right lane Bridger had just vacated, and the vehicle behind Bridger followed it over. The path between them now clear, the dark van surged forward, edging so close, Bridger thought the driver might graze his truck's bumper before he sped up a little more.

Bridger made to switch back into the right lane, ahead of another truck. His exit was coming up. He slowed just enough to keep the van in the lane and not anger the drivers behind him. He held his speed until the last possible second and then braked to exit, hanging the dark van out without a chance to exit from the left lane.

Or so he'd thought.

Tires squalled as the van braked and swerved in between two cars behind them. Multiple sets of brakes sounded, along with a couple of horns, but the van managed to make it to the exit ramp just as it met the shoulder again. Angry at nearly being outmaneuvered, the driver sped up and rammed into Bridger's bumper.

"What—" Sophie threw a hand out toward the dash as Bridger fought to correct the fishtailing truck.

"He's trying to put us in the ditch." Bridger held tight to the wheel as the van gained speed once more behind them.

An oncoming car blocked the merging lane he needed to enter at the end of the exit. He couldn't slip into traffic without slowing down more than he already had. He had to hit the brakes hard. He tried to swerve over onto the shoulder, but it wasn't enough.

This time when the van made contact with the rear of the truck, it sent them sailing into the ditch beside the exit ramp. The truck hopped and bounced when it landed in the steep decline of grass alongside the exit where the dirt had been moved at one time to build the ramp. Thankfully, the cab remained upright when they came to a stop at an odd angle in the hollowed-out ground.

"Are you okay?" Bridger tried to watch for the van and check on Sophie at the same time.

"Yes, other than a bit of a jolt from the impact. Where's the van?" She looked around and gestured about the same time he spotted it.

Bridger had already drawn his SIG and lowered his window by the time a man dressed in dark clothing opened the driver's-side door of the van. Bridger fired off a warning shot that hit the side panel of the van and the man dropped low for a second before advancing on them with a gun of his own.

Bridger fired again, this time targeting a leg, but a car whizzing off the freeway distracted him just enough to throw off his aim.

"Can you get us out of this ditch?" Sophie spoke in a quaking voice.

"It's worth a try." He ducked back into the cab and put the truck in four-wheel drive before easing the gas pedal down. For a moment, the tires didn't budge, but then spun for a minute before one caught at last, throwing mud at the gunman as he fired off a shot toward the truck. A thud sounded on the back fender just as they were launched out of the ditch.

Horns honked as Bridger wove into traffic, making room where there had been none. Sophie held tightly to the handle on the right side of her head but made no sound. As soon as

Bridger had the driving situation under control, he called for backup. He hadn't seen the man in the van coming after them yet, but Bridger had no doubt he would.

"I think you've lost him." A note of relief touched Sophie's tone.

"Good. Hopefully, there will be enough of a law enforcement presence at the scene to prevent another attack." Bridger eyed his mirrors before sweeping into a turn lane.

But his relief was short-lived. They were just reaching the disaster scene when the distinct sound of sleet hitting the windshield accompanied the tiny crystalline chips settling across the surface to melt.

"Oh, great. I thought we still had a couple of hours before this was supposed to hit." Sophie put her hands out in a gesture of disbelief.

"Who can predict Texas weather?" Bridger shook his head.

A man wearing a neon vest stopped them as they pulled in, his head ducked low beneath his coat hood against the sleet. Bridger showed his badge but the man shook his head. "I'm sorry, but we're clearing everyone out because of the weather, per orders from incident command."

"We won't be here long, but I need to clear a crime scene." Bridger scowled at the man. "A murder."

The man took a step back, surprise taking over his face. "So it's true then."

"I'm afraid so. We need to get what we can before this worsens." He gestured vaguely at the cloud heavy sky.

"Go ahead then, but better make it fast. Temps are dropping quickly." The man stepped back with a wave.

Bridger hadn't realized how frigid the air had become until they stepped out of the truck to make the short hike to the scene. Sophie shivered in response as she pulled her hood up over her head to shield it from the ice, and he knew her jacket was far too thin for the weather conditions. She had probably expected to have finished working the scene long before this weather hit. He mentally berated himself for not noticing sooner and vowed to make quick work of the job and get her some warmer clothing as soon as they had the chance.

"What can I do to help?" Sophie slowed as they reached the place where she had discovered the victim and he wondered if she was reliving what she had seen. The body had been removed to the morgue, but he knew the images in her memory wouldn't disappear so easily. At times, when he closed his eyes, he still saw images of disturbing things he had witnessed.

He handed her a pair of gloves. "You can help me search for anything that might have belonged to Agent Benton. Her personal belongings. Specifically, like electronic devices, handbag, items of clothing with pockets, or just anything at all suspicious. Trust your gut. If you see anything, give me a yell."

Her only confirmation was a nod. They moved off in opposite directions, eyes roving the ground as they occasionally bent to move debris out of the way. Nothing but rain-soaked ruins turned up for a while.

Bridger made sure to collect a sample of the suspicious liquid he had noticed earlier and was about to call it when he noticed Sophie was studying something a few yards away.

"Did you find something?" He made his way closer.

"Maybe. I think this is a flash drive." She wiped some mud away from a small piece of red plastic with her gloved fingers. He pulled a baggie from his pocket for her to drop it into.

He gave her a nod. "It could be nothing, but we'll check it out." The wind gusted, carrying some of Bridger's words away. The sleet began to intensify then, a few actual snowflakes mixing in now. Time was running out.

A UTV approached, driven by a man in a neon vest, and Bridger walked over to it to hear the man better above the noise of the engine. He still had to yell over the tinkling of the ice pellets rapidly striking the ground and the UTV.

"Best clear out and get somewhere warm. Roads are getting slick." It was the same man who had greeted them when they'd arrived.

Bridger thanked him and waved. "We're about to leave."

"Let me give you a lift. We all need to get home." His expression said he had warned them but wouldn't shirk his duty to make sure everyone was safe.

The shelter of the UTV provided a welcome relief from the ice at least, and once they reached Bridger's truck, the heat would ease Sophie's shivering. He only hoped the flash drive she had found would tell them something useful.

The traffic was almost nonexistent as they made their way onto the freeway, but a thin layer of ice covered the pavement where the little pearls of sleet had melted on the warm ground and then refroze as more ice continued to fall. It was slow going to try to get back to the ranch, early winter darkness already falling.

Just outside of town, however, a vehicle appeared in Bridger's rearview mirror. "Come on. Surely this guy doesn't plan to chase us in this weather."

Sophie looked startled as she turned to look at Bridger. She twisted to see behind them, though, and after a couple of seconds, confirmed his assessment. "I think it's the same van from earlier. He's relentless."

Bridger's head throbbed. This wasn't at all what they

needed on the slick roads. Likely, the guy thought the weather improved his chances of doing them in while making it look like an accident, though he might just do himself in at the same time. "I'm going to turn around. If he thinks I'm letting him follow us to the ranch, he'd better think again."

But they both knew the man on their tail probably didn't intend to wait that long to attack. When Bridger slowed to turn, the van's passenger window rolled down to reveal the nose of a gun, just before shots began to ping off the bumper. Sophie squeaked but didn't let out a full scream.

"He's not alone. Hold on, this could get rough." Bridger slammed on the brakes, embracing the skid, knowing the van would have to do the same. He turned into the skid, thankful he had learned long ago how to manage a vehicle in these conditions. Growing up on a ranch had meant caring for animals in all kinds of conditions, and an ATV wasn't all that different to handle on the ice than a full-size vehicle. As boys, he and his brothers had tested their skills to the point of near injury many times, but it gave him confidence now.

The van's driver wasn't as skilled at handling the icy roads, however, and he slid and skidded haphazardly for several seconds. He came close to sliding right into them at one point, but then missed them by a few scant inches. Bridger had been holding his breath the whole time. The van had now come to a stop, so Bridger pulled his weapon to fire back. Rolling down the window and hit with a blast of seemingly arctic air, he had to catch his breath before taking a shot.

Aiming carefully, he popped the front driver's-side tire before the men could shoot back. The driver tried, however, but Bridger targeted and struck the other front tire just as the passenger took aim, causing his shot to go awry as the van bounced in reaction to the blown tires. Then Bridger eased on the gas, straightening his tires to get moving before the van could recover.

The van's passenger attempted a few more shots, but Bridger accelerated carefully, soon taking them out of range. It wasn't as quickly as he would have liked, but it worked. He was glad for the four-wheel drive that minimized slipping as he made his way from the now-disabled van.

"That should slow them down for a while." Bridger let out a deep breath.

"That was close," Sophie choked out as they slid back onto the road. "If he had hit us, we could have easily been sitting ducks."

Bridger nodded, thinking she was right. The snow wasn't deep yet, but the slick ground in the ditches and on the sides of the road likely would have made the tires spin. Often a wrecker would be necessary to get a vehicle back on the road in these conditions. It would have been too late for them by the time a tow truck arrived.

Bridger offered up a silent prayer of thanks as he carefully maneuvered them back toward the ranch. He also asked for protection and guidance, two things he would desperately need until this was over. He breathed deeply, silent for the moment as they drove toward home.

Sophie's shoulders drooped and Bridger knew she was likely as weary as he was feeling right now. He released a long breath as the turnoff to the ranch came into view. They would make it in by dark, but just barely. The wintry sky made dusk fall quickly this time of year.

However, his relief was once again thwarted. As they turned onto the narrow two-lane road leading to the ranch, shadows loomed on the horizon up ahead. The deep gloom made it difficult to see what was ahead of them until they got closer. When he could make out the vehicle, he recognized the compact car that belonged to an elderly neighbor stopped along the road. He slowed carefully.

"Mr. Brownley, what are you doing out in this weather?" Bridger muttered under his breath as he put the truck in Park.

His question was answered when he noticed the position of the elderly man's frame in the car. Richard Brownley was slumped over.

"Oh, no. Is he all right?" Sophie realized the man was unconscious as soon as they pulled to a stop, and she was unbuckling her seat belt as Bridger opened his door.

"He was recently diagnosed with dementia." Bridger paused to explain before stepping out of the truck. "That's likely why he didn't stay in with this weather going on."

Sophie reached his side as he was trying to elicit a response from the elderly man. "What can I do?"

"Go ahead and see if you can get a call through to emergency services. He has a pulse, but his breathing is shallow and he's pretty cold. Let them know he's unresponsive." Bridger continued to examine him.

Sophie was relieved to get Dispatch right away, and once they had promised an ambulance, she returned to Bridger's side to help. "Does he have any other medical conditions that you know of? Diabetes, pacemaker, asthma? And it's awfully cold to leave him sitting out here in the elements."

She realized her words sounded hurried when Bridger looked up and blinked at her. She slowed down to await response. The car wasn't running and it was very cold inside.

"Come to think of it, he may be diabetic. Can you check

to see if he has insulin somewhere in the vehicle, and I'll work on getting him to the truck, where it's warmer." Bridger gestured toward the console of the car. Then he glanced at the dash. "It looks like he may also be out of gas. We may also need a tow truck."

"I'm on it." Sophie began to rummage around inside the car's console and found the insulin a moment later. "Bingo. Maybe he took too much if he had a bout of dementia. He could have forgotten he had already taken it or something."

Bridger nodded agreement. "That probably also has something to do with the lack of fuel. He was likely either confused because of the dementia or had brain fog from the low blood sugar. Either way, we can help paramedics out when they arrive by giving them somewhere to start."

"Let me help you get him into the warm truck. I'm stronger than I look. When Kai was a puppy, she was a real handful on a leash." Sophie raised one of her brows before rubbing her hands together.

They carefully managed to transfer Mr. Brownley into the truck to await the ambulance and called for a wrecker once he was settled. They were told the tow truck might take some time due to the inclement weather. All they could do then was wait.

"How well do you know Mr. Brownley?" Sophie asked the question to attempt some conversation. But she was surprised by his answer.

"Not that well, really. He's a neighbor, but a little reclusive and known by most to be a grumpy sort. We know enough about him to look after him." He gave a rueful chuckle. "If rumors are true, he probably wouldn't return the favor. He's a bit of a scrooge."

"But you helped him anyway." Her heart warmed at the thought.

"Of course. That's what neighbors do." He shrugged as if it wasn't even a question.

"I take it he doesn't have any family close by?" Sophie's thoughts turned to her mother, who was probably missing her presence right about now.

"Who knows? So many families aren't as close anymore. At one time, everyone took care of family, but it doesn't seem to be as common as it used to be. He may have no one. But he may have alienated himself on purpose." Bridger looked off into the distance.

Most of the ice falling from the sky had turned to snow and it picked up intensity just then, big white flakes falling as if in slow motion from the endless dark void above. It made Sophie feel like the rest of the world was very far away.

Until she remembered someone was trying to kill her.

Helping Bridger's neighbor had provided a welcome reprieve from her own problems. She vowed to remember that the next time she became too consumed with her own worries.

The ambulance arrived only a little before the tow truck and Bridger helped the paramedics, insisting Sophie to stay in the warm truck as the medics loaded Mr. Brownley onto a gurney. She watched him interact with them after they had the elderly man in the ambulance and realized with a jolting impact how easy it would be to fall in love with Bridger Cole.

She was going to have to proceed very carefully until they got this case resolved.

Bridger had returned to the truck and was putting on his seat belt when an officer in a heavy coat and wearing a toboggan waved him down. He rolled the window down, heedless of the snow, and greeted the man, obviously someone he knew.

"Just heard from Dispatch that they found the van that ran you off the road earlier. It was reported stolen, and when officers found it, the perp had abandoned it outside of town. It was clean. Nothing to ID the guy. Only prints from the owner." The officer's face was ruddy with cold, his expression grim. He nodded politely to Sophie, who returned a hello.

"Thanks, Gunnar. I'll check in as soon as we get back to the ranch." Bridger didn't seem surprised. "Y'all be safe out here and let me know how Mr. Brownley is, if you hear."

"Will do. Take care." The officer gave another nod before backing away from the truck.

When they finally arrived at the ranch, it was abuzz with activity. Kai greeted her with a wildly wagging tail as soon as Sophie entered the house. The smell of simmering cider permeated the air and the soft glow of white lights from the Christmas tree softened the living room.

Bridger introduced Sophie to his younger brothers, Campbell and Stetson, who were eating a quick dinner in preparation to go out to relieve other officers working accidents in the winter storm. They looked up with grins and nods as Bridger spoke.

"It's a team effort at the local level. And things have been unusually busy lately with this wild weather." Bridger did the explaining as his brothers scarfed down their dinner. "Campbell works as a deputy for the county sheriff's department. Stetson is a patrol officer in Oak Ridge."

Both young men smiled at her as they rose almost simultaneously with their empty plates. "Nice to meet you, ma'am."

"Better watch big brother, here." Stetson socked Bridger

in the arm with his free hand as he passed by. "The ladies seem to think he's a real charmer."

Bridger's face turned pink.

"Not true. He's too grumpy to charm anybody. They just chase after him anyway. Nobody really knows why." Campbell made this quip from the sink where he was rinsing his plate.

"Don't listen to them, Sophie. They're known storytellers." Bridger scowled at them both. "Hurry up and go get to work."

But Sophie could see they were all teasing, and their banter continued until Caroline came in. Then the three men teamed up against their sister.

"See what I have to live with?" Caroline turned to Sophie. "Come on. Let's get you warmed up."

Dana appeared from the hallway then and together they ushered Sophie off for a warm shower while they prepared a plate of hot food and a mug of cider for when she returned.

Less than twenty minutes later, Sophie entered the living room to find Bridger quietly staring into the fireplace over an empty plate and a mug of coffee. He looked up when she came in and motioned for her to sit down by the fire. Kai gazed at Sophie from a nest of blankets near Bridger's feet amid the corgis, who were lounging closest to the fire.

"Mom has your plate and cider ready." He rose to head toward the kitchen.

She stopped him. "I can go get it." But he waved her away and kept going. She heard him speaking softly to Dana for a few seconds before he returned.

"This looks amazing." Sophie's stomach growled in appreciation as Bridger handed her a plate with roast beef, potatoes, carrots, green beans and a yeast roll. It was the kind of meal she had grown up on and it brought comfort to her soul.

"There's apple crumb cobbler, also. Just fair warning." Bridger grinned.

"Thank you." She smiled back as she took up a forkful of the tender beef. "Your family is great."

"They can be a real pain sometimes." He winced. "Except for Mom, of course."

She put down her fork and gave him a thoughtful look. "I hate to ask, but..."

"My father passed away about eight years ago. That's why we all still live here with Mom. None of us had the heart to leave her after he died. We know we will all have to eventually, and she keeps telling us to move on with our lives, but it just hasn't happened yet." Bridger didn't meet her eyes for a long moment, just watched the multicolored warm flames dance in the fireplace. When he finally looked at her, Sophie could see how painful it was for him to talk about his father.

"So you've kinda become the father figure for your younger siblings." Her tone was thoughtful.

"We try to keep things as normal as possible between us. Try to behave as brothers should. But it's a little odd sometimes." Bridger took a sip from his red-and-cream reindeer mug. The pattern on it reminded her of a Nordic sweater.

"My father passed away when I was pretty young." Sophie took a bite and swallowed before continuing. "So I guess we have that in common."

She thought he might not reply, but finally he asked her to elaborate. "Mind if I ask what happened to him?"

Sophie considered the fragrant steaming liquid in her own mug before responding. She had told the story many times, but it never seemed to be right, always like she was leaving out an important truth. She supposed that was just how it felt to miss someone and struggle with losing them.

"He worked in a rock quarry. There was a terrible accident one morning and he was buried alive. Before anyone could find him, he died in the rubble. They said they didn't know if he had died right away or not. They might've saved him had they been able to find him sooner."

"Do the circumstances surrounding your father's death have something to do with your decision to volunteer on search and rescue crews?" He set his coffee down on the table beside his chair and peered at her thoughtfully.

She nodded. "My mother remarried eventually. I have two stepsiblings—a sister and a brother. But her second husband divorced her a few years ago and we don't hear from either of my stepsiblings much at all. They blame my mother and me for things going awry. My family is nothing like yours."

Bridger looked down at his large hands for a moment, where they rested on his knees. "I'm sorry to hear that. My family's truly a blessing. I forget sometimes that not everyone has this." He lifted one hand to make a sweeping motion around the room.

"My mother and I are much closer now, but it was often difficult growing up. She often sided against me to keep peace, even if I was in the right. She's apologized for it many times since, but there was still damage done." Sophie lowered her eyes to the food cooling on her plate, but she didn't really see it.

"I understand that." His eyes held such empathy and kindness when Sophie looked up that her eyes welled with tears. She sure couldn't mention how she had grown up in an old single-wide trailer with hand-me-down clothes and sometimes little to eat when things got especially tight.

Kai, either sensing her emotions or picking up on Sophie's tone, had risen from her curled-up position on the rug and now laid her big furry head on the cushion beside Sophie, nearly bumping her head on the plate as she did. Sophie responded by rubbing her ears gently.

"You'd better eat." Bridger straightened and rose. "No doubt your food is getting cold."

Sophie watched him walk back to the kitchen, though, wondering all the while how she was going to avoid falling for Bridger Cole.

FIVE

Bridger couldn't fight his restlessness any longer by the time the roads were mostly cleared the next afternoon. The major roads had been salted and plowed and he was ready to get to work. With no news yet on anything from the lab, he decided they should head to his office and check out the flash drive.

"We'll head back out to the storm site when we're done there, just in case we missed anything." Bridger pulled on a warm coat in case they were gone until late and temperatures dropped once more. "We can take Kai this time and maybe we can locate some of Agent Benton's belongings."

Dana insisted on Sophie taking one of her heavy winter coats until they could get her something of her own. She had apparently also realized how ill equipped Sophie had been for the weather yesterday evening. Sophie gratefully accepted it and gathered her things as well as Kai's for their mission.

As it turned out, the flash drive was encrypted with something Bridger couldn't access, so he sent it to their tech specialist, still unsure it was even important. Frustration filled him. The longer it took to sort it all out, the longer Sophie would be in danger. And against his better judgment, he was enjoying the time he spent with her more and more as the hours went by.

Earlier that morning, as he had listened to Sophie banter with his family and seen how kind and helpful she had been toward his mother, he had realized just how easily she could fit into his family. And more than that, how much he enjoyed having her there as a part of it.

It seemed his brothers had realized it, too, for on one occasion he had noticed Campbell grinning at him with a twinkle in his eyes before turning with a knowing look toward Stetson, who had given Bridger a wink.

Reining in his errant thoughts, Bridger helped Sophie load Kai into the Jeep to head out to the disaster site. He planned to stop somewhere along the way and get Sophie some warmer winter clothing of her own, since they seemed destined to be out in it until everything was resolved. He could see that she was a little uncomfortable having to borrow things from his mother and sister, and it was the least Bridger could do considering what she was going through to help him get to the bottom of this case. She hadn't brought much along in the way of luggage, likely thinking her stay at the tornado site would be short.

Though they had taken Sophie's Jeep this time to accommodate Kai, Sophie insisted that Bridger drive in case they encountered any more trouble. So far, it had been almost eerily quiet. But he wasn't dropping his guard.

He noticed Sophie was fidgeting a bit nervously, so he decided to try some conversation to distract her from her anxious thoughts. "You've told me about your mother and your stepsiblings. Did I hear you tell my mother earlier today that you're widowed?"

The question had been bothering him since he'd overheard their discussion. He told himself it didn't really matter, but it was something more they had in common if she had lost someone she'd loved. He and Jamie might not yet have been married when he'd lost her, but he had loved her just the same.

"Yes." Sophie said softly. "Troy had colon cancer. We'd been trying to have a baby, and things weren't going well, so we both went to see our family physician. He requested a full workup on Troy after asking him a few questions. By the time they found the cancer, he was already stage four."

"I'm so sorry, Sophie." Bridger reached a hand across the console to comfort her.

"I suppose it was for the best that we never had a child. I'd be raising him or her alone. But sometimes I still wish I knew what it was like to be a mother." Sophie smiled sadly.

"It's not too late." Bridger squeezed her hand. "I assume the doctors didn't find any reason to think your health prevented a pregnancy."

"No, everything was okay. But I don't really plan to remarry. I haven't even dated. It's too painful to lose someone like that. But what about you? Did helping to raise your younger siblings discourage you from having a family of your own?" Sophie turned the topic away from her reluctance to try a relationship again.

"Not at all. It was…other things. I had a serious girlfriend a few years back. Her name was Jamie. I planned to get her a ring that Christmas, but I was working a case locally and though I thought I had my bad guy, he wasn't working alone, and I didn't know it. He somehow found out who she was to me and kidnapped her, trying to get a deal for his partner before he was sentenced. I was impatient and wouldn't wait on my team, but instead I tried to rescue Jamie on my own. Things went terribly wrong. She was killed." Bridger choked out the last three words. The memory of seeing Jamie go down was a permanent scar in his mind. "I almost lost my job because of it as well. In the end, my supervisor decided I had suffered enough."

Sophie gasped. "Oh, Bridger. I'm so very sorry. You know what I'm feeling then. I think losing someone suddenly like that would be even worse than knowing what's coming. At least Troy and I got to cherish the last of our time together, though it was bittersweet. You lost her so suddenly."

"I won't say I didn't learn a lot from it, professionally as well as personally. And it was definitely a lesson I won't forget. But I've never really forgiven myself." Bridger sighed.

"I'm sure it wasn't your fault." Sophie was shaking her head.

"Not completely. But I'm still working on forgiving myself. It took me a while to forgive God as well. But we're back on good terms now." Bridger sent her a slight smile. "I couldn't have made it through without Him."

Sophie agreed, but they both fell silent in thought for the next several moments.

Once they arrived, Bridger provided a piece of Agent Benton's clothing from her last moments from an evidence bag—a scarf—and Sophie let Kai sniff it before giving her the command to search. Sophie had informed him earlier that Kai had been trained in both air scenting and trailing. The dog seemed to understand what was expected of her almost instinctively. Bridger was amazed by Kai's intelligence and abilities.

Snow still collected in a few shadowy places around the disaster site, but most of it had melted away by the time they'd arrived. The heavy equipment crews had been working again at some point, for large piles of debris had been scraped up at various junctures, clearing some of the ground for walking, though nothing had been touched at the crime scene. It was a punch to the midsection to think of how many people had lost so much as he stared at all the wasted belongings mounded up like so much refuse.

Turning his thoughts from the hills of waste, Bridger watched in wonder as the canine sniffed her way around, going to where the body had been found, ears drooping, and then morosely continuing on her way.

When she began to wander far off from the house foundation where Agent Benton had been found, Sophie's brow furrowed.

"Where's she going? I know tornados carry things a pretty long way sometimes, but it wouldn't have moved along the ground." Sophie followed her.

Bridger walked that way as well, curiosity filling him. But his phone rang.

The lab must not have been too busy. It had been only late yesterday evening when he had dropped off the liquid sample to be tested. "Hi, Vickie. What've we got?"

"Definitely accelerant. But not your typical gasoline or diesel. It's some sort of mixture with turpentine, but I got curious about the other compounds. I found traces of ephedrine as well. I suspect it was a chemical mixture someone was using to make methamphetamines. Just conveniently used it to try to start a fire." Vickie's voice sounded matter-of-fact, despite her comment. "The guy must have really needed to start a fire quickly."

Bridger considered her revelation. She was right, though. It was probably an expensive waste of product from the drug producer's point of view. Bridger, on the other hand, was glad to have any small amount of drugs off the streets.

He agreed with her, thanking her before disconnecting.

As soon as he was finished with the call, his phone

buzzed again. It was the boys from the crime lab sending a text. They had apparently found nothing in the red sedan, either. It had indeed been Agent Benton's vehicle, but no prints other than her own had been discovered. It was a disappointing dead end, but one he had pretty much expected.

He was about to go tell Sophie what he had learned when Kai began barking loudly and aggressively. His head jerked in her direction as it hit him what she had smelled.

"Sophie!" He couldn't get out more than her name before the man lunged from behind an overturned SUV half buried by rubble.

Sophie managed to dodge her attacker's grasp long enough for Kai to get between them. Kai let out a vicious growl before barking several more times. The man backed away from Kai as Sophie sprinted toward Bridger, who had pulled his SIG.

The would-be assailant took one look at Kai's bared teeth and then turned to see the weapon in Bridger's hand before he took off running in the other direction. Kai followed. Sophie allowed Bridger to push her gently behind him before calling Kai off. The dog came back to Sophie's side as Bridger commanded Sophie to get behind something and bounded off in pursuit of the man.

"Stop! Police!" He yelled the command but to no avail. The man disappeared around a mound of debris and then reappeared for a moment before disappearing again.

Bridger couldn't chase him much farther without leaving Sophie vulnerable, but he couldn't stand the thought of letting him get away again. He had to do something quickly.

Kai leaned into Sophie as they watched the pursuit, fear for Bridger pulsing through Sophie. He fired a shot toward the other man's feet, but it only made him run faster.

Sophie was beginning to think the chase was futile when the other man misjudged a step and stumbled over some storm debris. He let out a shout of surprise, and before Sophie could react, shots came from another direction.

"Sophie, get Kai and duck behind that wall!" Bridger called the directive over his shoulder, motioning toward a section of a house still partially standing to her right.

She scanned the scene for a moment before taking Kai with her to crouch behind the wall he had indicated. The shots followed them, grazing the wall and sending brick and mortar fragments spraying over their heads.

For a few moments, they hunkered there alone, fear filling Sophie as she waited blindly. For what, she wasn't sure. Safety? Bridger's command?

But then Bridger ducked behind the wall with them, instantly creating a sense of calm and comfort she was afraid to attempt to examine. His warm scent, spicy and masculine, enveloped her as he neared.

"Okay?" Bridger glanced her way before leaning around the wall to take a look. Another bullet struck with a dull clunk just as he ducked around the bricks to safety. Sophie winced.

"Yes." She emphasized her reply with a nod. Kai whimpered her own response.

Looking around behind them, Sophie realized they were also shielded by a mound of debris nearly as big as a two-story house. She could only assume it had been raked into a pile by the large, heavy equipment run by cleanup crews and she was thankful it was still there to help give them shelter.

"I think there are only two shooters." Bridger had his SIG in his hand, though he gripped it loosely at the moment. He leaned against the wall beside her, looking as if this whole situation was no big deal.

Her own heart thudded against her rib cage like it needed to escape. It had only slowed a little since the first man appeared, even after finding shelter behind the wall.

Bridger grasped her hand and a new type of racing pulse took over as she looked into his turquoise eyes. He checked his gun and holstered it for the time being.

"Is that good? That there are two of them?" Her voice shook and the teasing note she had intended to inject into the comment was lost.

Bridger smiled. "Better than three or four?"

Sophie nodded but couldn't quite return his smile. "True."

"I've radioed for backup. Just want to keep you safe until then." Bridger rubbed Kai behind the ears as she leaned into him for comfort. How easily the dog had grown to trust him, Sophie realized.

Another shot grazed the top of the bricks and exploded into a busted-up television in the pile behind them. Sophie jumped at the racket it created, but Bridger squeezed her hand. She had almost forgotten he held it while he rubbed Kai's head with the other.

But the shots kept coming and he released her hand. "I think he's trying to cause that pile of debris behind us to avalanche."

Sophie noticed then that the last two shots had hit close together near the television on the pile. A few bricks and boards had begun to splinter and slide a bit and, gradually, a few other chunks of debris started to wiggle and fall. Little puffs of dust rose up here and there as the pieces settled back into place.

Sophie's chest seized up with fear. Thoughts of her father

being buried in the rock quarry froze the blood in her veins. How long had she had nightmares about being buried alive, or seeing her father buried and being unable to help him?

She had spent years in therapy trying to overcome it before finally becoming able to work on a search and rescue team. But now it seemed she wasn't quite over it.

She must have appeared as pale as she felt, for Bridger grasped her gently by the shoulders. "Are you okay?"

Sophie nodded mutely, but as another shot fractured a chunk of concrete into pieces, the whole mountain of refuse began to skitter and slide toward them. They had nowhere to go. If they ran out from behind their shelter, it would give the gunmen an open shot.

But if they stayed...

Her lungs refused to make proper use of the air and sucked it in desperately and ineffectively. She was beginning to hyperventilate, something she hadn't done since her teens over a decade ago.

"Breathe, Sophie. Nice and slow. Count to ten. Hold it. You're okay. Let it out slowly." Bridger released her as she began to calm and pulled out his SIG once more. "I'm going to distract them while you and Kai get to safety, okay?"

Sophie nodded, but they had hesitated for too long. Gunpowder stung her nose over the dank smell of wet belongings, but she only noticed it subconsciously. The sound of slipping and creaking gave an ominous warning as it picked up in intensity. She looked up, making little sense of the waste piled before her that was shifting before her eyes. From somewhere in the pile, a child's toy began to play music and babble out something unintelligible. It was so eerie it gave her chills.

In a sudden quaking motion, whatever was holding the

debris came loose as if a dam had released the waters of a flood.

Sophie could only watch, frozen, as the rubble tumbled rapidly toward her. Another shot and she screamed, but it only worsened matters.

Bridger tried to push her away as the avalanche of wreckage broke loose, but Sophie grabbed for Kai at the same time, nudging her out of the way.

A chaotic storm of noise, dust and confusion was all that registered before everything went black.

SIX

Bridger pushed aside a mass of debris, every part of his body aching in protest while he fought to get his footing above it all. It shifted and moved with every step and he had to work at staying balanced, almost like trying to walk on a tightrope.

Where was Sophie?

He had tried to push her out of harm's way, but her thoughts had been on saving her dog. He couldn't see Kai, either, and though the avalanche had stopped for now, it might not be over.

"Sophie? Sophie!" He called out to her over and over, but there was no answer.

Clutching blindly at debris with both hands, he tossed it aside, coughing between breaths. He couldn't even see well in the haze of dust.

Finally, he heard a whimper. "Kai?"

The dog whined two more times and Bridger followed the sound to where she was wedged between some concrete and a piece of broken furniture. Shoving the wood cabinet away from her, he called to her. Kai bounded out, but began to limp slightly as she, too, began searching for Sophie.

"Where is she, girl?" Bridger knew the dog wouldn't need any commands to find her master. And they *would* find her. He couldn't consider the possibility that they might not get to her quickly enough.

The gunfire had stopped and Bridger could only assume their assailants had fled after causing the avalanche. He kept digging through the debris, looking for any sign of Sophie and watching for any little bit of movement.

Kai, too, chirped and whined as she sniffed and searched, finally focusing on a specific spot. She dug at the pile with both front paws for a moment. Then she sat back, looking at Bridger imploringly.

Bridger wasn't entirely sure what it looked like when a SAR dog alerted, but he thought the sharp bark before she'd sat on her haunches was definitely meant to tell him something.

As Bridger climbed over to where Kai waited, she whined once more, pawing at a wad of cloth tangled into some splintered boards. Curtains. He realized from the gathered edge that the fabric had once been curtains. His chest tightened once more with a pang of sympathy for the storm victims and all they had lost. He couldn't imagine what they must be going through.

But Kai hadn't barked to tell him to check out the curtains, so he tugged them aside, snagging the fabric on a splintered board before finally tugging them free. Carefully pulling them out of the way and picking up a piece of wood from who knew what, he found Sophie lying in a heap that made the breath catch in his lungs.

"Sophie." Her eyes were closed. Discarding the board, he began trying to look her over, but Kai was frantically licking her face.

Still, Sophie didn't respond. Her stillness sent a chill through Bridger. He reached for her wrist and leaned in close.

He sighed in relief when he found a pulse, but her pale skin and the shallowness of her breathing made him anxious to get her out of there. Before he could begin to uncover the rest of Sophie's still frame, however, Kai stepped back and let out two quick barks.

"What is it, girl?" Bridger looked up about the time he heard it. The debris was beginning to loosen, giving way from the towering mound once again.

They didn't have much time to get out of there before it all came crashing down.

Everything from splintered pieces of furniture, lawn care equipment, children's toys and nearly fully-intact building materials such as timbers and Sheetrock made up the small mountain. There was plenty to bury them.

Urgency sent his adrenaline into a spike as he began to shove the wreckage off Sophie, all the while calling to her trying to get her to wake up. Kai, too, licked and nudged at her master before attempting to dig away debris with her paws.

"Come on, Sophie. I really need you to wake up. I could sure use your help to get us out of here." Bridger only glanced toward her face, though, as he kept pulling the pieces of destruction away. The rubble above their heads taunted them, sliding a bit here and there, and then pausing, only to repeat the process over and over. It was just enough to keep Bridger guessing as to how long they had before the rest of it tumbled down.

But he knew it was coming down, sooner or later.

Kai barked another alert and this time there was no warning. Like a waterfall, everything began to move at once.

"Sophie!" He grabbed at her around the waist, tugging in desperation, but her legs were still somehow lodged.

Letting go, he began to shove at the debris around her feet and legs. Kai barked persistently now.

"Bridger?" Sophie's voice was weak, but one of the best sounds he had ever heard.

"Can you move your legs? We have to get out of here." He gestured up at the monstrous mound, the slide picking up speed.

Her eyes widened and she jerked upright. "I think so."

Sophie still sounded groggy, but not like before. The sight was enough to jolt anyone awake. She was already beginning to wiggle and kick slightly with her legs. She fought with every bit of energy she had. That was making it difficult for him to help her, though.

Bridger spoke close to her ear. "We're going to have to work together. When I say go, try to get your legs free."

She stilled for just an instant, but when he gave the word, Bridger latched on to her waist again as she took a deep breath and this time jerked her legs free as he pulled. At first, he thought it wasn't going to be enough, but finally Sophie's legs came completely loose. The avalanche intensified then.

"Kai, go!" Sophie gave the order, and the dog whined but obeyed. She didn't move far, though, waiting for Sophie a few yards away just in case.

The fury reached the bottom then, unleashing just as Sophie and Bridger tumbled out of the way. They had cleared only a half a second before the small hole in the rubble they had just occupied was buried beneath the mess. Dust from the mutilated Sheetrock flew everywhere and the musty stink of damp, weathered debris filled the air. Bridger coughed from his place beside Sophie where he had barely managed to deposit her on a patch of grass just beyond the chaos.

"Kai." Sophie was looking around desperately, tears already welling in her eyes.

"She's here. She's fine." Bridger released a breath of relief as the big, furry dog loped around from the other side of the dust cloud, tongue lolling to one side as she stopped next to Sophie to sit and bark. This time in reprimand to her owner, if Bridger wasn't mistaken.

"Oh, I agree, girl. That was too close." Sophie wrapped her arms around the dog and closed her eyes. Kai whined her agreement. Then Sophie looked up at Bridger. "Thank you."

"Don't mention it." He felt a rush of heat fill his face. "Are you okay? You must've hit your head pretty hard to be knocked out like that."

"It *is* throbbing, honestly." Sophie put her hand up instinctively and he saw the knot growing above her temple.

"We need to get some ice on that. It probably needs examining as well. Let's get moving. Nothing good is happening here." Bridger stooped to pick her up.

She threw a hand up. "What are you doing?"

"Getting you to the Jeep." He drew back. Surely, she didn't think he was going to expect her to walk.

"I can get myself there." Her jaw clenched and her chin lifted.

"I'm sure you could, but I'd rather not risk you passing out on me again." Bridger picked her up before she could protest further. "I'm just doing my job."

But as her warmth against his chest sank into him, tenderness filled him and he admitted to himself that he had never enjoyed his job more.

Sophie squirmed a bit in Bridger's arms. He might be just doing his job, but it was having a much more personal effect on her. His grip was filled with a gentleness she hadn't experienced since losing her husband over two years ago. Tenderness softened the strength of Bridger's tall frame, so she had to force her thoughts away from the longing to be held and cared for that his embrace incited. She had forgotten how nice it felt to rely on someone other than herself.

Kai followed along beside them, so when she stiffened and let out a low growl, it sent a shiver through Sophie that had nothing to do with the chilly December wind.

"Who's there?" Bridger paused. She assumed to listen.

Of course, no answer came, only a gust of wind blowing across the flat landscape.

Ducking behind some piled debris once more, he gently set Sophie down. "I think I'd better get my SIG ready."

At that second, a figure dressed in gray clothing shot toward them. He knocked Bridger off balance and pounced on Sophie, nearly toppling her to the ground.

Her scream echoed endlessly across the devastated landscape with no one else there to hear. Kai went on the offensive then, sinking her teeth into the attacker's forearm, causing him to drop a pistol that had been in his hand. He yelped in pain, and while Kai had him busy, Sophie struggled to free herself, making sure to kick the gun farther away in the process.

Her head throbbed, but she did her best to ignore it, pushing the much heavier man with all her might. Bridger had jumped to his feet once more and rushed into the fray.

Sophie rolled out of the way then and allowed Bridger and Kai to subdue the man. Their attacker was soon face down while Bridger cuffed him. Kai stood on point beside him, a warning growl rumbling from her chest.

Sophie's breath came in gasping pants. Bridger restrained her attacker as she looked on, feeling a bit like the whole incident had happened to someone else. She got to her feet slowly, holding a hand to her head. She took one limping step forward and realized her right leg had suffered more damage than she had realized. She nearly lost her balance before returning her weight to the left foot with a wince.

"Easy, there." Bridger hadn't missed her misstep.

"I'm all right." But despite her assurance, Sophie's ankle and knee both ached furiously on her right side. She took a few halting steps, trying to walk it off, and eventually it eased.

When police pulled up a few minutes later and loaded the man in gray into their unit, Sophie finally relaxed a bit. She called Kai to her and ran her hands over the dog's silky black, white and brown fur to make sure she was okay while Bridger finished up with the other officer.

"Thank you, girl. You saved me." She crouched beside Kai and leaned into her, letting Kai lick her cheek to see for herself that Sophie was fine as well.

"Twice today, actually." Bridger moseyed over to them with that unhurried, long-legged stride Sophie was coming to appreciate too much.

"What do you mean?" Sophie cocked her head to one side.

"When the pile of debris first covered you, I couldn't find you. She did. Kai led me to you. Who knows how long it might have been before I found you on my own, since you were knocked out and couldn't hear me calling to you." Bridger also gave Kai an affectionate rub.

Sophie smiled, but it faded as she watched the police car drive away. "What about the other guy? Weren't there two?"

"The officers are still searching, but there's been no sign

of him so far." Bridger gestured toward the remaining two police vehicles sitting along the edge of the disaster scene. "He's probably long gone, but they've suggested we get out of here and leave them to it."

Sophie nodded, more than happy to comply. She led the way to the Jeep and loaded Kai inside while Bridger followed silently.

"We're going by the ER before we go back to the ranch. I want to make sure you didn't get a concussion when you got knocked out earlier." Bridger had waited until they were back in the Jeep to tell Sophie this.

"I'm fine, Bridger, really." She waved his concern away. "A little Tylenol and I'll be good as new."

He insisted, though. "You may be, but we're going to find out. Just to be sure."

Bridger pulled into the hospital in Oak Ridge a short while later, helped Sophie out of the Jeep, and then let Kai out the back. He held on to her leash as Sophie led the way through the double glass doors of the emergency room to check-in.

They were there far longer than Sophie would have liked, but the emergency room doctor on call eventually pronounced Sophie free to go after explaining that she had a very mild concussion and informing her that she should take it easy for a few days.

As they drove back to the ranch in the quiet, she let her thoughts drift to happier things than the day's attack. She missed her mother, though she had called her that morning as soon as she'd woken. Admonishing her to be careful, Georgia had also expressed her hopes that Sophie would be home in time for Christmas. Sophie's heart had ached at the sadness in her mother's voice. She knew Georgia was lonely. Though her mother had never said so, Sophie was sure that she still missed Sophie's father, Curtis, terribly, despite her attempt at another marriage. It made Sophie wonder about Georgia's true feelings for her stepdad.

Glancing over at Bridger, she wondered how much of the budding emotions she felt around him were the same as what her mother had felt for Curtis Wilder. Were they the same or similar? Sophie had loved Troy deeply, but her feelings for him had been different from what she felt for Bridger now. Maybe at one time she had felt this same attraction and joy just being near him? But she remembered her feelings for Troy as more of a comfort, like being with a good friend. Was that love? Or was it what she felt for Bridger now?

She barely knew Bridger, of course. But the desire to *get* to know him was powerful. The tender feelings she had for him were deepening with each passing hour, and she couldn't deny that the longing to be with him again was strong any time they were apart.

And as they arrived at his home, she thought of his family and all the kindness they had shown her. It was such a warm, inviting place, the Cole ranch. She felt so content and at home there.

Before she could suppress the thought, she sighed into the realization.

She wanted to stay forever.

SEVEN

Stetson and Campbell had been caring for the horses and putting out hay for the cattle for the last several days while Bridger had been so busy, but today he relished the thought of taking Sophie out to see the animals and clearing his head of all the recent events for a short time. They could both use the distraction. When he asked her if she would like to go out to the barn with him, however, he was surprised by her enthusiasm.

"I'd love to. I always wanted a horse when I was a little girl. It wasn't possible, though." Sophie shook her head sadly, piquing his curiosity.

"Your parents didn't like animals?" Bridger asked.

To his surprise, her face turned pink. "It wasn't that. Horses are expensive. We didn't exactly have money to spare for something like that."

Realization dawned. What she didn't say told him everything.

"We didn't always have so many financial blessings. My parents worked very hard, my father especially."

Sophie ducked her head. "I'm afraid it took everything my mother made to keep us afloat. When she married my stepdad, things didn't improve a great deal, especially after two more children became part of the family. I was never even allowed to have so much as a cat. Another mouth to feed was simply out of the question."

"There's no shame in being poor." Bridger suddenly understood, though, why her relationship with Kai was so precious to her.

"No." Sophie tilted her head to the side to think for a moment. "The shame is in being unwilling to work hard for better things for your family. We lived in an old, single-wide trailer that my mom had paid for before meeting my stepdad. He was content with that."

"I see. Did your stepdad have trouble keeping a job?" Bridger asked, hoping he wasn't prying too deeply into her personal affairs.

"He did, mostly because he was lazy. He called in sick to work a lot, even when he was healthy. He would eventually lose his job and collect unemployment, and, after a while, he figured out how to abuse the system. He would botch interviews on purpose, just apply for the job and go to the interview to show he had tried to get a job. That was all they really required at the unemployment offices." Sophie frowned. "It drove my mother to distraction."

"I can imagine it did." Bridger handed Sophie her coat. "Not to interrupt, but we'd better get on out to the barn."

"Oh, of course. There really isn't any more to it. As soon as I was old enough, I got a job and tried to help out, even paying my own way through college. But it was never enough for him, and he finally left, supposedly because of my mother's nagging at him over his lack of employment. I honestly think it was more because all of us kids were grown and he could live more cheaply on his own." Sophie grimaced.

"It sounds like your mother is better off without him." Bridger slid into his own coat and replaced his usual cowboy hat with a thick toboggan, which he pulled down over his ears.

"Sadly, yes. I think she would get along well with your mother, though. They seem to have similar interests. And Mom always did her best to make things special with what little she had. I have a feeling your mother would do the same. It's obvious she adores you all." Sophie zipped her jacket up and nodded to show she was ready to go.

"That's pretty spot on. Actually, my mom did a lot for us when we were kids that I didn't fully appreciate until I was grown. I'm sure it wasn't always easy for her, though. Her parents were pretty well-to-do, but when she married, they told her she would be responsible for herself. Not because of anything she had done, but they believed a couple should make their own way in the world. It was more of a tough-love ideal, I guess." Bridger led the way out the backdoor.

"Oh, I know what you mean. It's like some say, growing together as you struggle together with making a home and family makes your relationship stronger. That sort of thing?" Sophie smiled at him for holding the back door for her.

"Yes, something like that. It seemed to work. I can only ever remember my parents being deeply in love. And they fully relied on each other for everything. They were true partners." Bridger led her across the yard then, cold wind nearly taking his breath away.

It had been unseasonably cold in north Texas since the tornado. Their winters were typically mild, but the past several days, highs had hovered in the low twenties, with overnight lows into the single digits. He hoped the cold spell was nearly over. He imagined the forties and fifties would feel quite balmy after this.

Sophie's reply was nearly carried away on the wind. "I'm sure she's just lost without him."

Bridger nodded agreement. "You're right, there. She's doing better these days, but it was tough for her for a long time."

They fell silent until they reached the corrals outside the barn. Bridger opened the biggest door on the barn wide enough for the horses to enter, advising Sophie to watch out for them. She understood why when the eager horses trotted by in a rush, pinning ears back at each other and whickering softly in their eagerness to get to their stalls. They reminded her of rambunctious children hurrying to be the first to get into the house.

"They know it's time to eat. They'll practically run a person down to get to the chow." Bridger laughed. "What they don't understand is if they trample me, there's no one to get their feed."

The horses each turned off into their own designated stalls as they reached them, some stomping and tossing their heads up and down as they waited for their dinner. Sophie chuckled at their antics, and Bridger encouraged her to pet one of the geldings who paused to sniff at her.

"You can pet him if you want. That's Charly and he's like a big puppy dog. Loves attention." Bridger began closing stall doors behind the horses.

Sophie rubbed Charly's nose and spoke softly to him, and Charly closed his eyes for a moment, enjoying the attention, before clip-clopping down the rest of the concrete alleyway to his stall, head bobbing with each step.

The warmth inside the large barn was welcome, and though they left the doors slightly cracked for ventilation at all times, the closed walls shielded them from the wind and the body heat from the horses warmed and scented the air. Bridger felt so at home here. And he couldn't help noticing how Sophie glowed with happiness here as well.

Sophie was admiring the horses, and he gave her a moment to walk through exploring, reading the nameplates along the stall doors and exclaiming over the beautiful animals. When she turned and smiled at him, he explained what they needed to do.

"Let's go to the tack room and ready the feed, then we can check water and put out hay last. It's a messy job if you aren't careful." Bridger gestured toward a closed door at the end of the barn's alleyway.

"Show me what I can do." Sophie offered her assistance with a soft, contented expression.

They finished up caring for the horses, and Bridger left Sophie talking to the animals as they ate while he took the small tractor out to place round bales of hay in rings for the cattle outside.

By the time he returned, Sophie's cheeks were pink and her eyes sparkled with delight. He gently pulled a piece of straw from her hair as she commented on her adventure. "That was fun."

But reality sank in for Bridger as they returned to the house.

Being a Texas Ranger didn't have all the advantages people thought it did, as he quickly remembered when he got back to work on the case. Soon Bridger had been on the phone for forty-five minutes just trying to get some answers. He couldn't go forward with this investigation until he could gather more information, but no one with the FBI seemed inclined to give him any. Everyone kept sending him to someone else because they weren't sure he had the "clearance" for the details.

He was beginning to think he was going to have to go to Bureau headquarters just to find out what he needed to know. But a trip to DC didn't sound at all appealing, especially this close to Christmas.

He was about to give up for the time being when a voice came over the phone, speaking his name. "Hello, Bridger. This is director Christopher Perez. I'm sorry they've given you such a runaround. We have to take security measures, of course. I have an agent in the field who will be coming to you. They should be there within the hour."

Bridger cleared his throat before speaking. "I understand, sir. Thank you very much."

"I'm sorry you had to get involved in this. I just want you to know we appreciate your help." Director Perez had a deep, authoritative voice, and when they disconnected, Bridger felt like he had just talked to a father figure. Hopefully, he would get the help he needed now.

It was just under an hour when the agent in question arrived. It was already dark out, so Bridger went to the door himself. He could see that the man at the door was a few inches shorter than Bridger was, but still the intimidating sort in his dark suit, broad shoulders emphasizing a serious face and closely shorn hair.

Bridger opened the door, introducing himself. The man returned the greeting. "Agent Ross McAuliffe. Nice to make your acquaintance."

Sophie stood, wringing her hands with uncertainty, in the corner of the living room when he motioned the agent inside. Bridger introduced her and explained that she had been the one to find Agent Benton, and motioned her forward, since she seemed unsure if she would be allowed to sit in on their conversation.

"Nice to meet you." Sophie smiled as she offered her hand to Agent McAuliffe.

"Benton was a friend of mine," Agent McAuliffe explained. "I didn't know she was undercover until she went dark. Then everyone started asking questions."

"So, she was working alone?" Bridger found that fact surprising.

"Not exactly. But the other agent she was occasionally making contact with wasn't due to speak with her for some time yet. They only made contact on rare occasions for safety reasons, and usually only if there was something to disclose." Agent McAuliffe shook his head. "It's a complicated situation. But her director was the one she had contacted last. They think someone suspected she was an undercover agent, or at least thought she was working with police."

Bridger's phone rang. "Excuse me for a moment, but this may be related to the case."

McAuliffe nodded as Bridger stepped out of the room.

"Detective Cole."

"Bad news. Your apprehended man in gray checked out as a hired hit guy. The other one was never found." The call was from the officer Bridger had spoken to at the scene. "I assume the one that escaped is the one the dog alerted on. This one couldn't be your killer."

Bridger frowned. He had told the officer about how Kai had caught the guy's scent on the scarf of the deceased and run him out of the rubble. But there had been two. Both dressed in gray. Both shooting at them.

"How do you know he couldn't be the killer?" Bridger suspected he knew, but he wanted to clarify.

"He had a solid alibi. He wasn't even in Texas the night before the tornado hit. We checked his plane tickets, financial records, all of it checks out." The officer made a sound of disappointment. "Trust me, we tried. Of course, he wouldn't talk about who hired him. Gave us some made-up name and swore that was all he had."

Bridger thanked the officer and disconnected, going back into the living room. Sophie's hopeful face turned up toward him, so he explained to her what he had learned from the phone call. "Just a hired thug. The real killer got away."

Her expression crumpled. "And Kai did so well."

"Who's Kai?" Agent McAuliffe looked confused.

"My search and rescue dog." Sophie gestured to where Kai lay curled up a few feet away, eyes watching Sophie. They explained how she had found Agent Benton and sniffed out the man in the tornado debris.

"She's beautiful. Could be a real asset to the case." He smiled at Sophie, the friendliest expression he had seen the man make yet.

Bridger felt a curl of something far too similar to jealousy roll up in his gut. Why should he care if the man noticed how beautiful Sophie was? It wasn't as if he had any claim to her. But when he looked at the man's left hand and saw no wedding ring, he had to admit he didn't like it.

Worse than that, he was almost angry about it.

Bridger reminded himself he needed to focus. This man was there to tell him what he needed to know about the case. He had to stop worrying about what other motives the agent might have and get what he needed to wrap this case up.

But when he and Sophie began talking about dogs and their personal lives, and really, things that had nothing to do with why the man was there, Bridger nearly lost his composure.

His tone was too sharp to his own ears when he cut in, folding his arms tightly over his chest.

"So, about Agent Benton?"

Sophie couldn't hide her surprised expression. She had never heard Bridger use that kind of tone before, and she could only wonder what had set him on edge.

She looked from one man to the other and found a vaguely amused expression on Agent McAuliffe's face, where Bridger seemed—well, *angry*.

Standing, she cleared her throat. "I think I'll make us some coffee."

Dana and Caroline had gone to a Christmas party this evening, and while Stetson was at work, Campbell was catching up on sleep before his next shift. That meant when the FBI agent left, Sophie would have the privacy to ask Bridger what on earth was wrong. But right now, she just wanted out of the room with the two men. The tension was just too much.

While she waited on the coffee to brew, she took down some mugs and set up a tray with cream and sugar, thankful that, before leaving, Dana had been kind enough to show her around and invite her to make herself at home. She wasn't worried about what the two men were saying, sure that Bridger would fill her in on whatever she needed to know later on.

Besides, she was getting a little weary of talking about the case and thinking about a murder. She wanted to forget while she could, take in the beauty of the giving season.

The glow of the white lights lining the outside of the farmhouse shone against the landscape just beyond the window, and Sophie wished for a moment that she could be there under different circumstances, baking cookies and singing carols with Bridger's family. Maybe even shopping with them and picking the perfect presents for each of them. She would have the groomer put a big red bow on Kai and take her out with them as they drove around looking at the Christmas lights. Perhaps she could even bring her mother for the holiday. How Georgia would love this ranch. She could easily see her mother chatting by the fire with Dana over coffee.

Sophie's imagination was certainly living it up.

Dana and Caroline had invited her to their Christmas party at the church, but Bridger hadn't thought it was a good idea. Sophie had to admit she agreed with him, and the last thing she would want to do would be to put other people in danger.

And she was also a little bit scared.

Bridger's protection made her feel a lot safer, but still, it was there lingering in the back of her mind, no matter how she tried to distract herself.

Someone was trying to kill her.

She wiped the thoughts from her mind once more as the coffeepot gurgled to a strong finish. She poured three mugs and settled them on the tray, taking a deep breath as she picked it up to return to the living room.

The expression on Bridger's face when he saw her returning to the room did something a little fluttery to her insides, but she looked down at the coffee tray instead. "I brought cream and sugar just in case."

She had poured the coffee into the three mugs she had prepared, and now she handed one to each of the men. When Agent McAuliffe accepted the coffee Sophie offered with a grateful expression and a word of thanks, Bridger's scowl returned.

She handed his mug to him carefully, hoping his foul

mood would diminish when she fixed her attention on him. It didn't.

As the men resumed their conversation, Sophie prepared her own coffee with a bit of cream and sugar before settling into a chair to listen. Kai was snoring softly, the corgis now snuggled up close to her side. It made her happy to see the incongruous trio looking so cozy.

"I don't have the name of her contacts, just the address where she was staying under an assumed name. We're hoping you can find something in her apartment." Agent McAuliffe gulped his coffee as if it were room temperature.

"And why doesn't the FBI just send in someone else undercover?" Bridger set his coffee on the table and stared the other man down.

Agent McAuliffe cleared his throat. "To be honest, we're a little short-handed right now. Agent Benton's death has exacerbated the problem. And we don't want to raise suspicion by sending in another newcomer to their midst. But the director over the case really wants to see this wrapped up. He has a personal connection, you see."

"What do you mean?" Sophie felt her brows draw together.

"His great-niece died at a college party. He believes someone slipped something in her drink that was laced with fentanyl. Her toxicology report showed traces of the drug along with alcohol and ketamine. Maybe someone was just trying to slip her a roofie, which is bad enough, but it turned out to be deadly." Agent McAuliffe looked angry at the thought. "It turns out similar incidents have been occurring all over the Dallas metro area."

Sophie nodded. "I've heard about some of them on the news."

"Agent McAuliffe has given me the address to the apartment where Agent Benton is believed to have been living." Bridger got to his feet, turning his attention back to Agent McAuliffe. "We'll check it out as soon as we can and let you know what we find. Is there anything else?"

"No, I think that about covers it. Thank you." Agent McAuliffe rose, as well, with a nod toward Sophie. "It was a pleasure to meet you, Ms. Wilder. And your beautiful dog."

Sophie smiled and returned the sentiment.

Bridger stepped closer to Agent McAuliffe then and extended a hand reluctantly before walking the agent to the door.

A short while later, Agent McAuliffe was gone and Sophie rounded on Bridger with a frown. "What was that about?"

"What was *what* about?" Bridger carried the now-empty coffee mugs to the kitchen, not pausing to hear what she meant.

"You were just short of rude to that man." Sophie had followed him and now stood in the open space leading into the kitchen, hands on her hips. He could play dumb, but she wouldn't let him off the hook so easily.

"I wasn't. It was just business." He still didn't meet her eyes. "And just because he flirted with you doesn't mean I have to be overly friendly to the man."

"He *what*?" Sophie couldn't help laughing.

"It really isn't funny. Pretty unprofessional if you ask me." Bridger finally looked at her. She could see then that he really was serious. She made a concerted effort to school her expression.

"I honestly just thought he was being nice." Sophie smiled.

"He's a federal agent. They aren't known for being nice." Bridger stomped out of the kitchen.

As she watched him go, Sophie couldn't suppress a warm, fuzzy feeling welling up in her middle at his reaction, ridiculous as it probably was.

Bridger had been jealous.

EIGHT

Bridger ran a hand through his hair. He had to get his head straightened out.

He needed to stop acting so ridiculous about another man smiling at Sophie, especially since they needed to get a plan together ASAP to check out Agent Benton's apartment. The sooner they could go, the less chance there would be of anyone knowing what they were up to. And right now, in the dark of night, would be the best time to stay as low key as possible. They wouldn't exactly be able to completely hide, but maybe they could slip in and out largely unnoticed. If anyone saw them at this late hour, maybe they could explain their presence as a simple visit to a friend.

Bridger stepped out onto the back patio, hoping the cold December air would help clear his mind. Stars twinkled down brightly in the night sky, making it seem as if it had been evening for a very long time. The soft sounds of the cattle munching on a bale of hay in the field just beyond were soothing and natural and the scent of horses was faint and distant as he breathed deeply of the fresh air. The bracing cold jolted him, but he was sure it hadn't wiped away the warm, cozy feelings he felt for Sophie. A vision of her swam in his head and he couldn't escape the dizzying emotions it provoked deep in his chest.

For a moment, he debated going to Agent Benton's apartment without her. He had no reason to believe she would be in any significant danger here at the ranch, since as far as he knew, the men who were after her didn't know where his family ranch was. Some time away from her might give him a chance to see things more clearly, and to remind himself why he didn't want to take a risk on loving a woman again.

But odds were, anyone could find it. It wouldn't take them a lot of digging to learn who he was, if they didn't already know, and make the connections to his family's homestead. They had a website, and though no pictures of the family were on it, it wouldn't take much to put it together. Sophie would be vulnerable without him.

So he couldn't—*wouldn't*—chance it.

Kai was another dilemma entirely, though. She could be helpful in many ways, of course. But it would be hard to go unnoticed with a huge Bernese Mountain dog in tow, and if anyone were to be watching Agent Benton's neighborhood, the dog would be a dead giveaway as to their identity.

She would have to stay at the ranch.

Decisions made, Bridger drew in one more deep breath of cold air and returned to the living room to find Sophie. He found her staring pensively into the blazing fire, having turned most of the lights off, and enjoying the glow from the flames and the Christmas lights softly gleaming from their nestled strands around the tree. She was probably wishing she was at home with her mother instead of there with him running from a murderous madman and his henchmen. Who wouldn't?

His heart softened for her just a little more in that moment. She hadn't complained. But it was less than a week until Christmas and she had no hope of going home until they figured this out.

It made him all the more determined to find something helpful tonight.

It was almost nine o'clock, but the lateness of the hour could work in their favor. Hopefully it meant no one would be about. If they could work out the details right, maybe they could get in and out of the apartment without being seen at all. And if they were noticed, they would just act like a young couple out visiting their friend.

Bridger sighed deeply before turning to reenter the house, knowing it could be a long night.

Sophie looked up from the fireplace when Bridger stepped back into the room and moved closer to her. His tone was gentle when he spoke. "Sophie, I think we need to go see what we can find in Agent Benton's apartment. I know it's getting late, but it's important we get to it before someone else does."

She nodded, her gaze still a bit distant and wistful. "I understand."

"I know you want to be able to go home soon. I'd love to get this figured out so you can."

He didn't remind her of the fact that someone was trying to kill her. From the shadows that entered her eyes at his words, he didn't think he needed to.

"Yes, my mother sent me a text a few moments ago. She sounds lonely." She rose to get her shoes, which she had kicked off to tuck her feet under a blanket. She folded it up and returned it to the large wicker basket his mother kept in the corner of the living room for such a purpose.

"Don't forget your coat and gloves. We might have to do some walking to keep suspicion down." Bridger moved to the entryway closet to grab his own coat, reaching in and handing her the warm down jacket his mother had loaned her earlier. He would tell her the plan on the way to the apartment.

She glanced toward Kai. "She's going to need to stay here again, isn't she?"

The sadness in Sophie's voice sent a pang of regret through Bridger, but he nodded. "I think it's best. She's pretty easy to recognize."

Sophie nodded her understanding. "Yes, she's difficult to miss."

A few short minutes later, they were headed toward the metro area in Sophie's Jeep, following the GPS directions from Bridger's phone. He connected to her Bluetooth system via an aux cord. Her screen showed the location of the apartment to be in a heavily populated area of the city, but it wasn't one Bridger was familiar with. He didn't like that news at all.

Sophie, too, seemed unsettled and anxious as she rode beside him in the passenger seat, her hands twisting and gaze roving their surroundings as he drove deep into uncharted territory.

He sincerely hoped they weren't heading directly back into the middle of trouble.

The December night air permeated the coat and sweater Sophie wore as she walked alongside Bridger down the sidewalk into an older part of town, fighting a shiver as the wind blasted her face. They were leaving behind the cheerful glow of Christmas lights and soft, jazzy instrumental carols wafting from boutiques and cafés as the streets turned dirty and unkempt on the outskirts of the city. She was surprised Agent Benton had lived so far into a sketchy neighborhood of the city, even if she had been working undercover. The buildings were crumbling, run-down, and in need of repairs, and the few shops and convenience stores around them had bars on the windows to prevent break-ins, as if they had been fighting off thieves for decades.

Sophie wondered, as she hurried to keep up with Bridger's long strides, if the location had more to do with what the agent might be able to observe in this area than the role she had been playing. A small cluster of teens and early twentysomethings eyed them with suspicion as they passed, and Sophie found herself wishing they had been able to bring Kai along for protection. Raucous laughter came from a dark alley nearby and Sophie's head jerked that way a little too forcefully.

Bridger gave her hand a squeeze, silently reminding her to stay calm. They were holding hands as they walked along the cracked sidewalk, hoping to look like a happy couple out for a stroll. Hopefully, news of what had happened to "Sarah," the pseudonym Agent Benton had been using according to McAuliffe, hadn't reached anyone in the neighborhood who had known her. Though, if someone had been watching her, they probably knew by now that she wasn't coming back.

"This is it. Third floor." Bridger whispered the words close to her ear before leading her toward a dilapidated apartment complex. A sign next to the speaker on the wall warned that though the intercom wasn't working, surveillance cameras still saw them.

Sophie followed Bridger's gaze up to where the camera perched, dark and still on the brick wall. He tugged her forward into the building as he offered up his assessment.

"I highly doubt that camera is functioning."

Sophie had to agree. No lights blinked anywhere on the camera and a tattered cord hung limply from the wall beside it. It looked just as useless as the intercom system.

Old varnish, cleaning chemicals and dirty socks scented

the air in the dim, run-down entry of the building as they crept quietly along the corridor. It was warmer, but that was the only kind thing she could say about it. Sophie wrapped her arms around her waist as she blinked to adjust her eyes in the darkness.

"Do you see the elevators?" Swinging her head around, she noticed where he pointed.

Bridger's grimace said it didn't matter. "We'll take the stairs."

She shadowed him through the corridor of the unusually quiet apartment building, wondering if that might have been another reason for Agent Benton's choice in lodgings. The stairwell stood at one end of the building, guarded by a heavy metal door at each level's landing, and a loud screech echoed through the dark cavern as Bridger pulled it wide for them to enter. It sent an involuntary shudder through Sophie.

When they reached the third floor, Bridger led the way out of the stairwell to apartment 317B. He knocked on the door but, just as expected, no response came. He produced the key Agent McAuliffe had given him from Agent Benton's locker and tried it in the lock. After sticking for a moment, it clicked open at last.

The apartment looked oddly empty, as if Agent Benton had already begun to clear out her things, and Sophie couldn't help peeking over her shoulder to ward off the feeling of being watched. An empty corridor stared back at her, just as barren and aged as the rest of the building.

"Do you think she left anything behind?" Sophie spoke quietly as the door slid shut behind her.

"Maybe. You take the bedroom and I'll search the living room." Bridger motioned to a closed door. "On second thought, let me take a peek inside all the rooms first."

Sophie waited where she was as Bridger drew his SIG and tiptoed through the small apartment, cautiously peeking into rooms and around corners.

Once he had cleared the tiny apartment, he replaced his SIG in the holster and they set to work searching. Sophie returned to the closet Bridger had already opened and began to dig through a couple of sacks of things lying in the floor of the small alcove. The closet held very little in the way of clothing, and only a couple of pairs of shoes. Either Agent Benton had been cleaning out her belongings to leave or she had brought very little with her on this assignment.

A double bed and a single nightstand holding a small lamp were the only bedroom furnishings, and it took her very little time to search the two nearly empty drawers of the nightstand. Nothing important caught her eye at first, but as she was about to close the second drawer, a photo stuck to the bottom underneath a small notebook drew her notice.

Pulling it out, she saw two young women staring back at her. They were smiling into the selfie, but only one looked sober. It was the only one she recognized.

Agent Benton.

Sophie shivered. How different she looked, alive and glowing with life. It made a swirl of nausea curl in her stomach.

She rose from her crouch next to the nightstand and carried the photo to the living room. "It's probably not what you had hoped for, but maybe this will help somehow?"

Bridger looked up from where he was searching under the cushions of an old cotton sofa and took the photo. "Agent Benton. But who is the other woman?"

Sophie shrugged. "I don't know, but if it's recent, maybe she can help us?"

Bridger nodded. "Let's finish searching the apartment and we will see if we can get any help identifying her."

Bridger pocketed the photo after studying it for a couple more seconds.

"I'll see if there's anything in the kitchen." Sophie left him to finish the living room, sparse as it was. Besides the sofa, there was only a coffee table and a television on a small stand.

The kitchen was nearly empty, also. A coffeepot and two mugs sat on the counter beside a microwave. Paper plates and plastic utensils occupied the cabinets, along with a few frozen meals in the freezer. Agent Benton clearly didn't make herself very at home on assignments.

Sophie opened the closet between the kitchen and living room to peer inside just as she heard a scratching and clicking at the door.

She froze.

Bridger, too, stuck his head around the bathroom door, clearly having also heard it.

He motioned for her to get into the closet and he drew his gun, hurrying over to where Sophie was.

The closet door snicked shut just as the apartment door rattled open.

"Put your hands in the air." Bridger spoke calmly to the intruder from the other side of the closet door.

A shot fired and Sophie sucked in a scream.

Who had fired? Was it Bridger, or was she on her own?

NINE

Bridger rushed the man in front of him before the criminal could get another shot off.

The bullet had gone wide, burrowing into the wall a few feet from Bridger's shoulder, but he wouldn't take the chance that the man's aim would be that poor the next time.

Bridger drove his shoulders into the newcomer's knees, knocking him off balance. The weapon slid from the shooter's hand, but he scrambled after it. Bridger leveled a punch at the side of his jaw as he did so, leaving the man stunned for a moment while Bridger knocked the gun away from his immediate reach. He holstered his own gun to subdue the man and try to cuff him, but the other man wasn't to be so easily outmaneuvered. Clawing out of Bridger's grip, the smaller man squirmed and managed to swing a leg out, knocking Bridger off balance.

The prowler jumped on Bridger then, but he managed to sling the guy off him and lunged at him again. Pinning him against the wall, Bridger held him there firmly.

"Who are you?" Bridger growled the words into the other man's face as he tightened his grip. "Why did you break into this apartment?"

The trespasser gasped and shook his head. Bridger relaxed his grip a fraction, allowing the man a little more room to breathe. "Well?"

"I came t-to check on her." The man squinted under Bridger's hold and then his eyes went wide. For the first time since he had burst into the apartment, Bridger really looked at him. He was young. Probably only around early twenties at best, if Bridger had to guess. "She was supposed to meet us at the party last night and she never showed up."

"Who are you? Who is *us*?" Bridger relaxed his grip on the interloper but didn't let him go entirely. He had fired a gun at him, after all.

"My name is Carter. Sarah and my girlfriend, Lydia, are friends. When she didn't show up at the party, we got worried. And she hasn't been answering her text messages for a couple of days." The young man actually looked pretty upset by the tale.

"Did you call the police? Check in with the apartment supervisor?" Bridger paused for effect. "Or knock before picking the lock?"

They both knew he hadn't.

"Look, man, I got scared. She's been acting funny lately and I was afraid she got in over her head, ya know? I didn't call the cops because I didn't want to get anyone in trouble." His gaze turned shifty.

Finally, Carter straightened in realization of what was going on. "Who are *you*?" He cursed softly. "You're a cop, aren't you?"

The fear on the guy's face told Bridger everything he needed to know. "You could say that. But if you cooperate, you don't have anything to worry about."

Carter didn't look so sure of that. "What does that mean?"

"Sit, Carter. Don't move." Bridger's tone left no room for argument.

Bridger tapped on the door and told Sophie it was safe to come out. Then he moved to stand in front of Carter. "It means there are a lot bigger issues happening here than a kid breaking into an apartment to check on a friend."

Carter looked dubious, like there was much more he was trying to hide.

Bridger raised an eyebrow. "Or shooting at an officer of the law with a stolen gun."

Heat flushed the young man's face and he looked over at Sophie. "Is she a cop, too?"

Sophie smiled, and she and Bridger both shook their heads. Bridger explained. "No, she's a friend."

Carter nodded. "Where's Sarah? Why are you here but she isn't? Did she have to leave town? Oh, man, she said they might catch up to her and if she disappeared, we should stay away. I really should have listened to her."

He was shaking his head, eyes on the floor. Bridger waited until he looked back up at him. "Sarah's... Well, she was found dead. Murdered. I don't suppose she mentioned who might be catching up to her, did she?"

"Murdered? Oh—" Another string of less-than-clean exclamations left his mouth before Bridger cut him off.

"That language is not necessary." Bridger looked pointedly at Sophie.

Carter ducked his head. "I'm sorry, ma'am."

"Who was she afraid might catch up to her, Carter? And for what?" Sophie gently prodded him to answer after accepting his apology.

Carter looked at her before turning his attention back to Bridger. "I don't know his name. But he supplied her... whatever she wanted. But sometimes people get behind on paying, and it ain't good, ya know? I mean you always think it won't happen to you, but if it does... Like I said, it ain't good. She never actually said that's what happened, but you assume things, ya know?"

"Would they kill her for owing them money?" Sophie's tone held the high pitch of incredulity.

Carter shrugged. "I've heard of it happening."

Bridger knew that wasn't what had happened to Agent Benton, and he knew Sophie was aware of that, too. But perhaps that had been the story Agent Benton had led Carter and Lydia to believe. He didn't want to give away too much. Letting Carter know he was law enforcement held enough risk. He couldn't let him know that "Sarah" had been DEA just yet.

He had to learn everything he could.

"I'm going to need to talk to you and your girlfriend a little more. I have a lot of questions for you. Can you get her over here?" Bridger wore the intimidating look of a man not to be reckoned with, but still, Carter hesitated.

"I don't like talking to cops. Am I, like, a suspect or somethin'?" Carter looked genuinely frightened.

"No, unless you give us reason to become one. But we need you to tell us everything you know about Sarah." Bridger fixed him with a hard stare.

Still, Carter was shaking his head, pressing his lips closed. "No way. I ain't sayin' nothin'."

Bridger pulled out the photo Sophie had found in the drawer. "Is this your girlfriend, Lydia?"

Carter paled, finally nodding. At this, he relented at last.

"I'll ask her to come. She's gonna be devastated, though. She and Sarah were so close. She ain't gonna believe this." Carter suddenly looked panic-stricken at the realization of what had happened.

Bridger glanced at Sophie, feeling out of his element when the kid's eyes began to tear up. Catching Bridger's eye, she stepped in.

"I know this is difficult. But we're trying to get justice for Sarah. Whatever help you two can give us brings us closer to putting Sarah's killer behind bars." Her voice was soft, and Carter responded favorably at first.

Until he panicked.

Carter shot up off the sofa like it was suddenly on fire. "I can't. I can't talk to cops. If they find out, I'll be next. And Lydia. It's too big a risk. No way."

He darted for the door and Sophie called out behind him. "Carter, wait!"

But Bridger put a hand on her arm. "Let him go. He'll come find us."

Sophie felt her brows furrowing on her forehead, and she wanted to insist that Bridger stop him. How would they find Carter again if he didn't? She voiced her concerns. "What makes you so sure?"

Bridger dropped his hand from her arm, looking at the place where it had been with a far-off expression. She was still wondering what was on his mind when he shook his head. "If he doesn't come forward, his girlfriend will. He said she would be devastated, so she's going to want to catch the killer. I think she'll take the risk."

Sophie shrugged. "I don't know. I mean you've never met her. She might be too afraid of being killed as well."

"Well, I guess we'll have to wait and see. Until then, we have some other places to look." Bridger motioned to the door. But at her questioning look, he pulled a piece of paper from his pocket.

An address stared back at her in messy handwriting, and

just below it, the word *party* in all caps with two exclamation points. She gasped, searching Bridger's face. "Where did this come from?"

"I found it under the sofa cushions. I didn't know if it would be important or not, but after Carter mentioned the party she didn't show for, I wondered if it could be." Bridger tucked the torn paper back into his pocket.

"That's not far away from here." Sophie had already typed the address into her phone's maps feature. "Only about a five-minute walk on foot."

Bridger looked over her shoulder at the location. "It's the opposite direction from where we parked, though."

Sophie shrugged. "Should we drive there?"

Bridger shook his head. "I don't want to risk being recognized. If Agent Benton was hanging out there to try to ID the leader, there could be someone around who recognizes your Jeep. But I'm going to let my brothers know where we are, just in case. Stetson will be on shift for a while yet, but he could send someone if we need them. And Campbell is a light sleeper. We all share our locations in case of emergency and he will check on us every so often."

Sophie wondered again what it would be like to have family like that. They not only got along, but they seemed to have each other's back no matter what. She started for the door while he sent the text.

Bridger made sure he double-checked the locked door before they returned to the smelly stairwell to leave the building. Tucking the key deep into his pocket, he grasped Sophie's hand once more and she felt a tingle of warmth move all the way up her arm and settle in her middle. His hand holding hers felt so right. How easy it would be to let her affections for this man grow into love, if only she could. Pulling in a deep breath, she forced her focus back to what they needed to do.

They walked at a brisk pace along the empty sidewalk, warming themselves in the process of escaping the cold night air, and Bridger tugged on her hand to slow her down as a rickety old warehouse came into view around a corner. The streetlights emitted only a weak light, and they were old and widely spaced in this area. He guided Sophie to a dark corner on the edge of an alley and gestured toward the warehouse, where a faint light shone from somewhere deep within. It was a large building, but only a newer chain-link fence on one side of the exterior indicated anyone had even frequented the place recently. Everything else about it looked pretty well abandoned.

"That's it. And it looks like there's activity somewhere inside." Bridger spoke in hushed tones, and Sophie hoped they were more alone than she felt. She hadn't been able to shake the feeling of being watched since discovering Agent Benton's body.

"Are you sure it isn't just a light left on for security? The place looks all but abandoned to me." Sophie wrapped her free arm tightly around herself, eyeing the long, flat building skeptically. She really hoped he wasn't going to ask her to go inside. Everything about it screamed *trouble* to Sophie.

"I doubt anyone would be worried about security here." He pointedly looked around the dirty streets. "And the local delinquents wouldn't be throwing parties here if there was a concerned owner keeping an eye on things."

Sophie had to admit he had a point. "Okay. So, what now?"

He summoned back her worst fear when he replied. "We're going to find a way in and take a good look around."

She shook her head even as he motioned that they should go around to the back to see if they could access the building. "I don't think this is a good idea. Can't we just come back when it's daylight?"

He chuckled softly. "Are you going to lose your nerve on me, now, Nancy Drew?"

Sophie shrugged, knowing he was right. But she had a bad feeling about this. "I suppose I am. I just... I don't like it."

"It won't take long. We'll be in and out in minutes and headed home." Bridger dragged her along gently now. "I won't let anything happen to you. But I need to see inside."

Bridger visually searched high and low as they snuck around the side of the structure. Just to be certain, he tried the door very carefully, in case anyone was inside to hear the latch click. It was locked. Creeping along the back of the warehouse, they spotted a broken window that, on closer inspection, was partially raised as well.

"There's our way in." Bridger dropped her hand and slowly and very carefully forced the window open a little wider, though she still wondered if his broad-shouldered frame would fit.

A few seconds later, however, they were both standing inside the dirty old warehouse. Bridger drew his SIG, guiding Sophie behind him as they made their way through the dust motes and scattered debris littering the concrete floor. The light glowed from somewhere in the center of the building, and Bridger followed it on near-silent feet. A strong odor of chemicals filled the air and Sophie fought the urge to gag. Bridger must have been fighting the same thing, for he gestured and pulled his coat up to cover his nose and mouth, indicating she should do the same.

As they moved deeper into the warehouse corridors,

Sophie shuddered as a rat squeaked and scuttled out of sight, but she managed to hold in her gasp. At the edge of a doorway, they came to a stop at last, the only illumination glowing just beyond the slightly open door of an oddly partitioned-off room in the center of the structure.

"Stay put. I'm going to peek inside." Bridger whispered the words very close to Sophie's ear, and she only nodded.

As Bridger stepped forward to look, however, a great groaning noise, followed by an ominous creak, echoed around them in the hollowed-out building. It was a heavy metal door opening somewhere close by, he realized as it slammed shut.

They weren't alone.

TEN

Bridger had only gotten the briefest glimpse inside the room before the metal door to the outside of the building had lumbered open, but it had been enough to see what was going on. The smell had provided a clue, but the paraphernalia and equipment crowded into the area had left no doubt.

This was where they had been making the drugs.

"We've gotta get out of here, now." Bridger gave Sophie a gentle shove, indicating the direction to go, farthest from the side entrance where the noise had come from.

Sophie hesitated, but Bridger grabbed her hand again and tugged her off at a run. They slipped once on a wet place in the corridor, but he didn't take the time to try to figure out what it was. A man's voice called out behind them.

"Who's there?" It was deep and angry, and no doubt the guy was armed to the teeth.

He was likely one of two things: the man in charge of manufacturing the drugs or the guard in charge of killing anyone who showed up there without authorization from his boss. Neither option was someone Bridger wanted to tangle with late at night in the middle of the sketchy side of town with no backup.

He briefly heard the man on the phone, telling someone what was happening.

Sophie's breathing came fast behind him but he urged her faster. A warning shot ricocheted through the corridor and it prodded her on more than his tugging hand ever could.

They reached the back door and Bridger tried unsuccessfully to open it, fiddling with the lock and trying to force it open with his weight, but it wouldn't give. The footsteps paused then repeatedly started up again, no doubt as he looked for them behind doors and corners, before pounding ever closer.

"Back out the window. Hurry." Bridger nudged her ahead of himself, and Sophie jumped up to throw a leg over the ledge as the voice yelled at them again. The window sat higher off the ground from the inside and her grip failed, causing her to slip.

Bridger folded his hands together to make a step and lifted her slight weight off the ground for her to get through the window as the footsteps skidded around the corner.

As Sophie dove through the window, their pursuer began to fire again. Behind her, Bridger jumped and dove headfirst through the window, but not before a bullet struck the outer edge of his left shoulder.

He let out a harsh gasp as the bullet tore through his skin, but he twisted his body as he fell through the window, managing to land clumsily on his right side before jumping to his feet.

"Keep running. Go!" He knew Sophie probably didn't need the encouragement, but he was afraid she was going to look up and see him bleeding and freeze. He ground his teeth together, threw his right hand over the burning pain radiating through his left shoulder and ran after her, ignoring the warm sticky liquid spilling onto his fingers.

They hadn't gone far before he heard the man running after them. It was only a matter of time before he had help. And if they were caught snooping around someone's drug lab, they were dead or worse.

They needed backup of their own.

He pulled Sophie into an alley and motioned for her to hide behind some dumpsters, struggling not to gag at the smell of rotten garbage and animal feces. She wasted no time pulling her jacket up over her nose again, blocking out what she could of the odors despite the struggle to breathe she was facing.

Bridger didn't have time for that. Ignoring his blood-covered hand and the pain radiating through his shoulder, he quickly sent another text to the group his brothers were in and asked for backup ASAP. He didn't take the time to give them any details, knowing they had his location and would respond with or without them.

Their pursuer's footsteps rounded the corner, and as they did, Bridger pointed the nose of his SIG around the edge of the dumpster and fired. The man yelped and jumped in surprise before ducking back around the corner. Bridger hadn't counted on the sticky, wet hand throwing off his shot, but it had. He had been aiming for the man's gun hand, to no avail.

"Let's get out of here." Bridger didn't bother to whisper this time. He pointed toward the far end of the alley, away from the other man, and Sophie sprinted off again like a track star. He had to admire her spunk just then. She'd been still gasping for air seconds before.

As soon as the man heard their running feet, he chased after them once more, firing off another shot just as they disappeared around the far corner. Brick and mortar dust flew behind him when Bridger glanced over his shoulder at the crumbling old shop they had just rounded.

Sophie slowed a few seconds later, looking at him for direction on where to go. He motioned for her to turn into the next alley, hoping for another temporary hiding place so he could get another shot at the guy. This time he would wipe his hand off first.

A lone SUV sat at the corner and Bridger checked it out to see if anyone was inside, thinking someone could be sleeping in their vehicle this time of night. He was surprised he and Sophie hadn't run into any homeless people before now, thinking about it. But no one seemed to be in the frost-covered vehicle. He debated for a moment before deciding to use it as cover, but the alley seemed to be otherwise devoid of shelter. He pulled Sophie over and they crouched behind it. Her eyes widened as she squatted down beside him and he realized she had just noticed his gunshot wound.

"You've been shot." Her quiet words echoed with horror.

"It's just a minor wound. Thanks to my jacket, it only grazed the skin." He didn't want to admit it still hurt like everything.

"That's a lot of blood. You might need stitches." She was shaking her head as if she couldn't believe his nonchalant attitude about it.

"It'll have to wait. We're kinda being chased by a killer. Or his henchman. Whatever he is, I doubt he wants to catch up with us just to chat." Bridger looked around the back bumper of the SUV. "Shh, he's coming."

This time when the man came into view, Bridger was ready. Their pursuer held his gun out in front of him with both hands, presumably to shoot first this time, but Bridger was faster.

He fired before the guy could spot him and heard a grunt of pain accompany the clatter of his Glock as it hit the concrete. He cried out.

Bridger stood then, SIG trained on the other man the whole time. "Don't move or it'll be your right leg next."

Shaking from the pain in his hand, the man put the other hand in the air. "Better just kill me and run. The boss is on the way. He'll make short work of you."

So, he was just a guard. "I doubt that. Who's this boss that you think is so powerful?"

The man laughed. "I'm a dead man if I say."

"You might be anyway." Bridger tried to persuade him with the cold hard truth. Working for hardened criminals typically came with a very short lifespan.

"I won't give him any more reasons." Blood soaked the man's shirt where he clutched his hand to his chest.

Sirens sounded in the distance then and Bridger knew his brothers had come through.

The man's head snapped up when he heard them, and in a blink, the tables turned and he fled. Bridger ran after him, calling over his shoulder for Sophie to stay where she was.

He considered shooting the man in the leg anyway. He wanted that badly to question him and get some answers.

But he'd hesitated too long and the man ducked into an alley just as the lights from his brother's police unit flared into view.

Sophie stared at Campbell's sheriff's department patrol Tahoe in a bit of a daze. She didn't know whether she was hot or cold; so much had happened this evening, she was still reeling from it all. Campbell had called for an ambulance and the paramedics had wrapped her in a blanket after she'd assured them she wasn't injured. Now she was just waiting for Bridger to be treated for his shoulder and take her back to the ranch.

"This is some case you're in the middle of, big brother." Campbell whistled low. He'd been grinning when he'd said it, obviously enjoying his job. And probably getting to rescue his brother for once, since he had mentioned when he'd arrived that it had always been the other way around.

Bridger was practically growling in annoyance as a paramedic cleaned his arm. He had filled his brother in while they'd waited, but he had argued that he only needed a bandage on his arm.

"I'll get a team together and we'll SWAT the place first thing tomorrow morning." Bridger and Campbell were still discussing the warehouse; how they could shut down the illegal drug production.

"You know it won't matter unless the ringleader is caught." Campbell shrugged, having been in law enforcement long enough to know situations like the one Bridger found himself in were never simple or easily resolved.

"I do know that, but it's a start. At least maybe it will slow them down for a while." He frowned, shaking his head. "We have to do whatever we can. And maybe somehow we can bring some justice to the family of the woman from the DEA."

They fell quiet for a moment, Bridger's expression practically brooding as he sat on the gurney. Sophie shoved her gloved hands in her coat pockets and waited. When Bridger's phone buzzed, he handed it to his brother.

"Looks like your flash drive only had a couple of names." Campbell told him. "Says they'll forward it all to the FBI, and you'll be briefed on it later."

"Sounds about right." Bridger grunted. He had hoped it was the breakthrough they'd needed to close the case.

Campbell, ignoring his big brother's bad mood, had been proven correct by the paramedic's announcement that Bridger was going to need stitches. That had only darkened Bridger's mood more. Sophie kept quiet, not wanting to make it worse, but another police vehicle pulled up just then, Oak Ridge Police Department emblazoned across the side. Stetson got out, and Bridger audibly groaned at the smirk on his face.

"Did you get *shot*?" Stetson asked as soon as he exited the patrol unit. His face was far more amused than concerned.

"Wow. Brothers really don't cut each other any slack, do they?" Sophie said in under her breath, but one of the paramedics standing close heard her.

The paramedic shook his head and shrugged before replying. "I have three brothers myself. They'd be doing the same thing."

Sophie just watched as the three brothers ribbed each other good-naturedly, carrying on about how Bridger had to be the first to do everything.

"I'd rather neither of you tried getting shot, if you don't mind. I don't really recommend it if you wanna know the truth." Bridger still looked angry, but Sophie could sense his mood lightening. She began to suspect the ribbing was actually for Bridger's benefit. As Stetson glanced her way and asked if she was all right, she caught a brief glimpse of the concern in his eyes that he was clearly trying to hide from his older brother.

"I'm fine, thank you for asking. Bridger took excellent care of me." Sophie pulled her hands from her coat pockets and accepted a hot cup of coffee from a female officer who had been on the scene earlier and gone to get it for them.

"Thank you." Sophie smiled gratefully at the female officer.

"Oh, hey, Nadine." Stetson greeted her as he recognized her. She wore a county deputy uniform, but Sophie assumed Stetson knew her through Campbell.

"Officer Cole." Nadine nodded at him, her tone guarded.

Interesting, Sophie thought.

But she didn't have time to ask questions or ponder the thought, for just then the paramedic declared he had done all he could for Bridger and it was time to go get him stitched up.

"I'll take him, since I'm finishing up my shift." Stetson motioned toward his SUV.

Bridger looked like he was about to argue when both brothers along with the paramedic took a step toward him. He sighed deeply. "Fine. Let's get this over with."

He hadn't made a sound while the paramedic had cleaned and bandaged the wound, and Sophie admitted to herself that his toughness was admirable. She had grown up in Texas. She was no frail flower, but she knew it must have been to be painful.

The trip to the ER didn't take as long as Sophie had anticipated, despite the lateness of the hour, but fatigue swamped her as soon as she settled back into the vehicle. It had been a long night and she just wanted to get some rest.

They swung by the neighborhood just down from Agent Benton's apartment on their way back to the ranch to pick up Sophie's Jeep they had left there. However, when they got back to the Jeep, smoke scented the air.

"Do you smell that?" Bridger looked at Stetson, who's scowl told Sophie all she needed to know.

Breathing it in once more, she realized why both men

looked so angry. It didn't smell like just any structure fire. Chemical residue scented the smoke.

"Is that...?" Sophie let it trail off, because no one had to point out the obvious when an explosion rocked the street a few blocks away. As flames shot high into the dark night, she felt her stomach clench.

The warehouse had been set on fire.

ELEVEN

It didn't take long for the adrenaline surge to kick in as the fatigue that had plagued him moments ago faded away.

Bridger had refused the pain meds the ER doctor had offered, only allowing him to numb the area with a local anesthetic before giving him twelve stitches, and now he was grateful. It looked like he was going to need to be clear-headed for a while yet tonight.

Sophie, though yawning a minute ago, was now staring wide-eyed at the blaze. The horns and sirens of approaching fire trucks filled his ears, even as he told Stetson to stop the SUV. A small crowd of people was beginning to gather along the rutted sidewalk several yards from the blast, but there was only one shadowy figure Bridger focused on.

The one running away, on the other side of the building.

He had just caught sight of the movement in the glow from the flames as the runner darted into an alley just out of view, but he was already jumping out of the vehicle to run him down.

"Bridger, bro, where are you going?" Stetson threw his door open to follow, though, even as he asked the question.

"He's getting away." Bridger shouted the words over his shoulder, knowing his brother would know exactly who he meant.

"Stay here and lock the doors." Stetson called the command into the SUV before tearing off after Bridger. "I'm pretty sure that's our guy since he's running away instead of towards help."

Laser-focused on the escaping arsonist, Bridger scanned for any sign of the fleeting man as he entered the alley where he had last seen him. He could hear his brother's footsteps behind him, catching up as Bridger slowed. He saw a glint of light off the end of a pistol just in time.

"Get dow—" Bridger couldn't be sure if Stetson had seen the glare from the gun. The echo of the gunshot cut off the end of his command, and the thunk of brick and cinder block where more bullets began to strike the wall came before the next volley of fire sounded.

Bridger and Stetson ducked behind the corner of the wall, listening to the metallic clink as the casings hit the ground just before running feet gave away the shooter's flight.

Stetson had his gun drawn. "I've got him."

Rounding the corner, he fired, but Stetson watched as the dark figure, clad in black, disappeared from the alley at the other end. But not before a grunt of pain.

"That should slow him down a little." Stetson glanced at Bridger.

They surged after him once again, seeing drops of blood glistening on the cracked concrete at the end of the alley. Bridger gestured to it and they followed the trail, creeping quietly forward as the spots slowly grew closer together. They disappeared into an alcove beside a building housing some sort of café. It was dark inside, so Bridger anticipated an attack as he got closer. He fired his SIG at the man as he jumped out to try to tackle him but then dodged as soon as he saw the weapon Bridger aimed at him. Glass shattered in the front of the café as Bridger ducked low to take the man out at the knees. He didn't have to struggle long before pinning the shooter down.

"Let's get some cuffs on him." Bridger had the guy facedown on the sidewalk and Stetson looked on with satisfaction.

The man was silent while Bridger read him his Miranda rights. Another officer hurried over to help hold the probable arsonist then. When Bridger finally got a good look at the face in the streetlight, he couldn't believe what he saw.

"Carter?" He couldn't keep the disbelief out of his tone. "You set the warehouse on fire?"

"He paid me to do it. I needed the money." His voice held desperation. "He just flashed all that cash and I couldn't say no."

Searching Carter's pockets, Bridger pulled out a wad of hundred-dollar bills. Counting it, he realized the guy was even more desperate than he had thought.

"Three thousand dollars? I'd say that's a pretty low rate for arson. You should've held out for more. Especially since you'll be going to prison for it." Bridger paused dramatically. "You should've let me cut you a deal instead."

"I'm still not talking." Carter shook his head stubbornly.

"I didn't figure you would." Bridger knew whomever it was this kid had ties to likely had people working for him even in prison. And it was obvious he had everyone who worked for him afraid to cross him.

"Hey, Bridger." Stetson called him over.

Bridger left Carter in the custody of the officer and made his way to where Stetson stood, feeling the burn intensifying in his shoulder once more from the increase in activity now that his adrenaline was tapering off.

When he reached his brother's side, a knot formed in his

stomach as Stetson's grim look registered. "What's happened?"

"The firefighters found a body." Stetson swallowed hard.

"In the warehouse? Deceased?" Bridger needed to know everything. Was it the guard? The ringleader of the operation?

"Yes to both. A young woman. Dead at the scene. Gunshot wound to the head, execution-style." Stetson's tone was flat, strictly business.

Dread swam up his spine. This sounded too familiar.

"I doubt this one was DEA, though. Sorority tee shirt, too young to have that much experience." Stetson shook his head as he continued. "And carrying a pillbox."

"Fentanyl?" Bridger's gut clenched at the thought.

"I suspect so. We'll send it to the lab to be sure." Stetson clapped him on the shoulder. "Go see about Sophie."

Stetson went to help the other officer keep watch over Carter while Bridger made his way back to Sophie in the SUV. When he told her what had happened with Carter, shock colored her features as well.

"I guess you were right about one thing. He did find us again. I'm just not sure he meant to do so." Sophie's face fell into a resigned sadness. "I really thought better of him. I'd hoped he had just gotten off on the wrong foot and could turn his life around before he got in too deep."

"Maybe he still can. If he can learn from this. Still, he'll go to prison for a while first." Bridger was shaking his head. He knew better than to be disappointed to find someone wasn't the person you thought, but he was human enough to still hold out hope for them all. "But there's more."

Bridger told Sophie about the body the firefighters had found in the warehouse and he could see her face pale, even in the dim streetlight. She shook her head sorrowfully. "This is awful. We have to put a stop to this."

"I completely agree. It needs to end before more lives are lost."

His words had barely trailed off when something caught his eye. A young woman wearing black clothing from head to toe, was easing away from the group of onlookers gathered at the edge of the scene. She was as slender and willowy as a pixie under her black stocking cap, and she moved with halting grace. The jet black hair that stuck out under the hat was pulled into two buns on either side of her pale face and heavy dark makeup made her features a little difficult to discern, especially at this distance, but there was something familiar about her.

Turning to Sophie, he saw she had noticed her as well. "Is that...?"

"The girl from the photo." Bridger finished her query.

"Lydia. It looks like she's dyed her hair." Sophie nodded. "I'm going to go talk to her."

Bridger laid his hand from the uninjured side of his body on her arm. "Wait."

While they watched, the young woman made her way closer to the police unit where they were loading Carter into the back seat, nervous energy apparent as she glanced around at her surroundings. Was she involved in her boyfriend's crimes, or just trying to see if he was okay?

A glint from the streetlight along her cheekbone took a moment to register, but when it did, he felt a pang of empathy for the girl.

She was crying.

"Do you think she knew what he was up to?" Sophie's voice wavered as she realized Lydia's predicament. No doubt, she wanted to go to him but feared being accused of something as well.

"I'm going to guess no, judging by her reaction. She seems kinda young and naïve despite her tough-girl appearance. Like she hasn't lived this sort of life for long." Bridger hated to make assumptions, but usually hardened criminals' girlfriends reacted with anger and rebellion, not tears and anxiety. "I'm going to say he's also probably a little new to this."

"New to being involved in criminal activity?" Sophie wanted to make sure he meant what she thought he did. She still wasn't sure what all that entailed.

Bridger nodded. "It might work in our favor. We might get her to talk if we offer her protection. She's probably pretty frightened right about now."

Sophie sensed Bridger's intentions, but she wanted to try to appeal to the girl before he tried police questioning. "Can I go talk to her before you interrogate her?"

Bridger hesitated for a few seconds before finally nodding. "I'll be right here, if you need me."

But before she could get close, she saw Lydia dart into the shadows. Trying to follow, she noticed where she was headed as she pulled the hood of her nondescript black jacket over her head. She hurried up to one of the police units and slid something under the windshield wiper then looked over her shoulder surreptitiously and darted away.

Sophie tried to follow but she disappeared into an alley. After searching for her for several minutes, she decided the young woman was gone, and returned to the police SUV to see what she had put under the wiper blade. The officers were still dealing with other things on the scene and hadn't seemed to notice.

A small slip of paper, folded neatly, opened to reveal a

short, cryptic message. "Tell the detective and his girlfriend to meet me at Sarah's place in half an hour. No tricks. Don't tell anyone else."

Girlfriend. The word sent a thrill through her for just a moment until Sophie remembered that's the part she had been playing. Lydia must have spoken to Carter before coming here.

Sophie slowly made her way back to Bridger and showed him the note, telling him what had happened with the girl.

"She's scared. I'm sure she's looking for protection. Her only protector probably just got hauled away in a police car." Bridger looked down the dirty street.

Sophie nodded her agreement. "Let's hope she can help."

When they arrived at the apartment a little while later, Bridger prepared to use the key but the door was already slightly ajar.

"She's here." Bridger whispered the words, gesturing to the crack in the door.

Sophie let Bridger lead the way to be sure it wasn't a trap, and then she went in, softly warning the girl of their presence. "Lydia, are you here?"

A soft footstep was her only answer before she peeked around the corner. "No tricks?"

"It's only us." Sophie closed the door quietly.

"Carter said you offered protection in exchange for information. I think I'm going to need some protection." Lydia turned, walked to the small kitchenette table and sat down.

Sophie followed and sat across from her. Bridger stood, giving her some distance, though near enough.

Lydia looked even younger up close. She was very dainty and petite, but she had a youthful, pixie face beneath the heavy makeup. She was staring off into space, a few tears still streaking her face here and there.

Sophie wanted to comfort the girl, though she restrained herself, knowing Lydia probably wouldn't accept it. But her skin was pale and her small white hands shook with emotion, inciting empathy in Sophie.

"My friend is dead. Actually, two friends now. And Carter's probably going to prison. I want this to end." Lydia's voice held surprising strength, a sharp contrast to the tears rolling down her cheeks.

"I understand." Bridger nodded, expression solemn.

"You can protect me? You're sure?" Her direct gaze remained level as she swiped at her eyes.

"The Texas Rangers will, for sure. You'll probably be placed in protective custody." Bridger paused, letting her come to grips with what would happen next.

"Like WITSEC?" Her eyes narrowed.

"Something like that. Although, that's the US Marshals Service." Bridger glanced at Sophie. She wasn't sure what for, but she assumed it had something to do with the fact that she was already under his protection.

Lydia looked at Sophie then. "Where's your dog? Aren't you the one who found Sarah? You and that big dog?"

Sophie exchanged another look with Bridger. Lydia sure seemed to know an awful lot about what had transpired over the DEA agent and who Sophie and Bridger were. His compressed lips and slight nod said he was thinking the same thing.

"Actually, yes. What do you know about that?" Sophie tilted her head to one side.

Lydia shrugged. "Just that Sarah was found dead after the tornado the other night."

"That's not really common knowledge." Bridger was in detective mode. He crossed his arms over his chest. "It's been kept out of the news."

"She was my friend. Word gets around." Lydia crossed her arms over her chest, also. She and Bridger eyed each other with suspicion.

Sophie felt compelled to intervene. "Sarah's death was tragic—"

Lydia cut her off. "So is Bailey's."

Sophie took a deep breath. She assumed Bailey was the young woman who had just been found in the fire. She exchanged a look with Bridger. How did she already know about that also? Sophie decided she'd better confirm her suspicions. "Is Bailey the young woman they found in the warehouse fire?"

Only a nod from Lydia, so Sophie continued. "Yes, it definitely is. And senseless. So, I think the best thing we can do here is to try to bring justice to their families."

"Sarah didn't have any family." Lydia shook her head.

"Well, her friends then. What about Bailey? Have you known her for very long?" Sophie had the sudden thought she might not make a very good detective. She didn't seem to be much help getting Lydia to open up and relax.

"I've known Bailey the longest. A couple of years. She has a sister in Dallas. Her parents are divorced and both live near Austin. She came here to get away from it all. The drama." Lydia waved a dainty hand around in the air as if to say it was obvious.

"Did she live alone here?" Bridger picked up the questioning once more.

"She had a...boyfriend." Lydia pressed her lips together slightly.

"And she lived with him? What's his name?" Sophie had a feeling *boyfriend* was a nice way of putting whatever the guy was to her friend.

Lydia hesitated and then seemed to remember that she

had come to them to try to help. "They call him Rocky. I'm not sure if that's his real name or just a nickname. And I don't know his last name."

That didn't give them much to go on. Sophie waited for Bridger to say more.

He studied Lydia's features for a moment first, presumably to gauge her honesty.

"Carter said something about a party a couple of nights ago. That Sarah was supposed to meet you there?" When Lydia nodded in response, Bridger went on. "Who's party?"

Lydia swallowed. "I'm not really sure but Bailey invited us, so I assumed it was Rocky's party. And he was... interested in Sarah, so he wanted her to come."

Sophie wondered what that meant. Had Rocky somehow been on to Sarah's real identity? Would Lydia know if he was?

Bridger continued questioning her, though. "Was this party held at the warehouse that just burned?"

Wide-eyed, Lydia gave a single, slow nod.

"Lydia, who lived in the neighborhood where the tornado hit?" Bridger was leaning toward her. "Why was Sarah there?"

"I don't know, honest. I heard it was her boyfriend. But someone else told me it was a friend of Rocky's. I don't know if either is true." Lydia threw her hands out in a gesture of surrender.

"What about the warehouse? What can you tell us about it?" Bridger quickly fired off the next question. The rapid change of subject would hopefully catch her off guard and get an honest answer. She had said she wanted to help, but her body language told Sophie otherwise.

"I... What do you mean? We had parties there sometimes. Just an old, abandoned building that no one cared about, so we hung out there." Lydia shrugged.

"Do you really believe that?" Bridger gave her a look that said he didn't think she was that gullible.

"Do I believe what?" Lydia looked at Sophie and then back to Bridger.

"The place has electricity. Do you think abandoned buildings have lights and running water? We know what was going on there, Lydia. People are dying from the drugs produced around here and this place could have something to do with it. Who was in charge of the drug operation?" Bridger's face had darkened.

She flinched at the mention of the fentanyl-related deaths. Did she know something more about that?

"I didn't ask those kinds of questions. I value my life more than that." Her face drew into a scrunched-up frown.

"I get that. But surely you've heard things now and then. I can't help you if you don't tell me what you know, Lydia." Bridger put both hands on the table in front of her and leaned close.

Lydia went perfectly still. "I want a deal for Carter. Get him off."

Bridger made a noise that sounded suspiciously like a snort. "He committed arson in an attempt to destroy evidence and fired shots at an officer of the law. A woman died in relation to the fire he started. I think he'll be lucky if we can get his sentence lightened. What was your involvement in his criminal activities, Lydia?"

Her face turned even paler, though Sophie wouldn't have thought it possible. "He didn't know Bailey was there. He's not a killer."

"That depends upon how you look at it, doesn't it? I mean how can you be sure?" Bridger looked angry. But he didn't tell her Bailey had been shot, and it seemed she thought her friend had died from the fire. "You say you want to help us, but you haven't given us anything. Not really. Just an ultimatum."

Lydia began to shake her head furiously, but Bridger continued.

"What do you think will happen if you go back home and word gets out you talked to cops? You need protection. But you're going to have to hold up your end of the deal."

Heavy silence weighted the air for several long seconds. Then a sigh from Lydia, followed by a rapid string of words.

"All I know is that Rocky is in charge of the manufacturing. He doesn't own the building, and he's the only one who knows who does. He's in charge, though, sort of like a manager, I guess. But he answers to the big guy. Whoever it is, he doesn't come around." She stopped and looked around like she feared someone else was listening.

"Do you know where to find Rocky?" Bridger asked.

"I don't know the exact address, but I think I could explain it. But I don't think you want to go there." Lydia shuddered. "He's not exactly a nice man."

"I kinda gathered." Bridger seemed to be barely suppressing a smile, despite the seriousness of the situation. Sophie supposed Lydia probably was understating the obvious in her youthful naïveté.

"How did you end up here, Lydia?" Bridger changed the topic once again. The implication was apparent. She didn't seem to fit in with the partying, drug-dealing crowd she found surrounding her, despite her appearance. She was intelligent and somewhat innocent considering the company she kept.

"My mom died. The state sent me to foster parents until I was eighteen, then… Well, I followed Carter out of town."

Lydia's tone had morphed into something more hardened, more resigned to life's unfairness. Though she presented the facts with blunt dispassion, Sophie sensed there was a lot of angst veiled beneath her practiced reply.

"And Carter? Does he have any family?" Bridger looked toward the small window where a light beam passed over. A flashlight?

"Just his dad. But he beat him on the daily, so Carter had to get out. He's twenty-three now, though." The way Lydia said it made Sophie think that Lydia must be barely over eighteen herself. Sophie had to reconsider her earlier thought that Lydia seemed innocent. Lydia had apparently seen a lot in her young life. "He would have left sooner, but he was waiting for me."

The beam of light passed over the window again and this time Sophie felt a twinge of unease. Whoever had killed Agent Benton knew her apartment should be empty. Could the killer be watching? Did he see the three shadows moving in the wan light beyond her window?

"Bridger, is someone watching?" She spoke just above a whisper, for Bridger was looking at the window again, too.

"It's possible. We need to get Lydia out of here."

Before he could follow through, however, someone began to rattle the doorknob and then the sound of a lock pick clinked in the silence. Bridger pulled his SIG and aimed it at the door.

Without hesitation, Lydia jumped up and dashed over to the window. Throwing it open as wide as the old sash would go, she climbed out onto the fire escape amid Sophie's protests and disappeared into the night, leaving nothing but the metallic sound of the lock on the apartment door clicking open behind her.

TWELVE

Bridger aimed the gun at the door, but before it swung open, he heard the sounds of a scuffle in the hall. He ran to the door and pulled it open only to see two male figures wrestling for dominance. One was in a police uniform and it only took a moment to recognize the taller man.

It was his brother Stetson. "Stop right there." Bridger's level tone made the two men freeze, but the shorter man, wearing dark clothing and a ski mask over his face, recovered first and fled to the stairwell.

"Stop!" Stetson called, running after him again, but the echo of the man's footfalls was already sounding on the stairs.

Bridger could only watch, unwilling to leave Sophie unprotected. Just moments after Stetson disappeared, the sound of a small motorcycle engine revving up met his ears before the squalling of tires followed. A very angry Stetson trudged out of the stairwell a bit later.

"He's gone. Not sure if the bike was his or he stole it, but I got a plate." Stetson grunted as if this was far less appealing than subduing and arresting the man.

"I don't suppose you got a chance to ID him?" Bridger holstered his gun at last.

"Nope. Sorry." Stetson's face didn't betray his anger, but

his tone did. "So I followed the suspicious-looking dude in the ski mask here from the scene. I still don't know what he wanted to break in for."

"Right. Well, he managed to scare off our informant. She just bailed out the window. You scared the wits out of her." Bridger shook his head.

"Hey, I would have just knocked. He's the delinquent who decided to pick the lock." Stetson gestured in the general direction of the man who had just fled. "Besides, I think we'll be seeing her again. Did you know the locals are having a memorial service for 'Sarah' tomorrow at ten? I guess some of the girls put it together to honor their friend." Stetson gave Bridger and Sophie all the details he had gathered.

"How did you learn all this?" Bridger asked when he was done.

"I was questioning some of the people who gathered at the warehouse fire. People are a lot more willing to talk when they're frightened. The recent events have many of them pretty shook up." All traces of humor were gone from Stetson's countenance now.

"Understandably so. Things are getting uncomfortable for someone and it seems that someone is out to destroy anyone in their way." Bridger motioned for Sophie to head toward the door. "Let's go home and get some rest. We'll come back at ten tomorrow and see what we can learn."

The next morning, when they tried to approach a few of the young people, however, the response turned out to be quite negative. Muttering circled the room before Bridger and Sophie had even fully entered. And they had even brought Kai, hoping it would make them seem more approachable.

"Have you seen Lydia?" Sophie finally whispered after many of the gatherers had turned away from their greetings, murmurs of *cop* echoing loudly as they turned to their friends. It sure hadn't taken long for word to get around about who they were.

"No, I haven't seen anyone I recognize at all." Bridger offered up a shrug.

Kai whined and a blond-haired young woman looked at the dog, her face softening a bit. She half smiled at Sophie when their eyes met, but then she aimed a fear-filled look at Bridger before moving away from them.

"Sheesh, they don't want to be anywhere near us. I feel like we've contracted the plague or something." Sophie snorted softly.

"They're all pretty young. No doubt most of them are afraid of arrest because of involvement with illegal drugs. Half of them don't even look like they are old enough to drink alcohol legally. They haven't developed into careless hardened criminals. But most of them likely will soon if they don't get their acts cleaned up." Bridger spoke in a quiet voice, but most of the group stood too far away to overhear anyway. He almost wished they would, if only it turned just one of their young lives around. He hated seeing so much wasted potential.

They remained alone in one corner of the room when a young woman moved to the front of the gathering and asked for everyone's attention. The crowd quieted as she reminded them why they were there. The group of young people turned out to be larger than Bridger had expected. A few of them grew teary-eyed as the young woman spoke about how kind Sarah had been to them all and how she had given them new hope in many ways through her contagious optimism.

It warmed Bridger's heart to see the positive influence the agent had exerted on these young people, even as she'd played a role working undercover. He couldn't help but wonder if Agent Benton had known what an impact she had made.

Just a few minutes after the young woman had begun to speak, Bridger noticed Lydia slipping in the back. When her eyes met his, they widened before she looked away, intentionally disappearing into the crowd. Sophie had noticed, too, and her head bobbed around as she silently tried to relocate the young woman.

As the short memorial drew to a close several minutes later, the young people began to file out, a few casting cursory glances at Bridger, Sophie and Kai as they passed. A few looked wistfully at the dog as they moved, but only one had the courage to pause.

"Your dog is so pretty. Would it be okay if I pet it?" It was the blond girl Bridger had noticed looking their way earlier. She was young, much like Lydia, but a weariness in her face put her a little older, in Bridger's opinion, whether physically or just emotionally, though, he couldn't be sure.

Sophie responded to the blonde with a warm smile. "You sure can. Her name is Kai. She's a Bernese Mountain dog."

"Wow. She's so soft." As the girl gently rubbed Kai behind the ears, the canine closed her soulful brown eyes in pleasure, her mouth falling open in a doggy grin.

"Mind if I ask your name?" Sophie kept her tone casual and light, and Bridger silently applauded her gentle approach.

The young woman hesitated. "I—uh…"

"It's all right if you don't want to tell me. We aren't here to frighten anyone or get anyone in trouble." Sophie smiled again and Bridger found himself nodding beside her.

The young woman glanced around, and seeing nearly all her peers had gone, spoke in a timid voice. "My name's Poppy."

"Nice to meet you, Poppy. I'm Sophie, and this is Bridger." Sophie offered the girl her hand and Poppy took it reluctantly, eyeing Bridger as if afraid he might want to shake her hand, also.

Bridger decided to step away for a moment then, hoping to see what direction Lydia had gone, and also hoping that if he gave them some privacy, it might encourage Poppy to talk to Sophie.

Stepping outside the small community building where the group had gathered, Bridger looked up and down the sidewalk lining the street, but if she was traveling on foot, she had already made it out of sight. He watched the people milling about for a few more minutes before stepping back inside.

Poppy's cheeks sparkled with fresh tears as her hushed voice beat out a quick staccato of unintelligible words. Sophie's head bobbed sympathetically, so Bridger assumed she could make out Poppy's words well enough standing as close to her as she was.

Unwilling to frighten Poppy out of sharing anything she would, he stepped back to the door to wait out of sight.

Several minutes passed before the door opened and Sophie and Kai emerged. Alone.

"I have a name."

She'd said it so quietly that he thought he'd heard her wrong at first.

He nodded. "Let's get out of here. Then you can tell me all about it. Where's Poppy?"

Sophie jerked her head to one side. "She slipped out the back. Didn't want anyone to suspect what she was doing."

Bridger hoped it was precaution enough to protect the girl, but he didn't offer Sophie any false assurances of that. "Good job with her, by the way. Bringing Kai along was a great idea. But we'd better get her home. I have a bad feeling about lingering here."

In truth, he'd had reservations about coming at all.

He was almost sure someone had been watching them the whole time.

Sophie sensed Bridger's apprehension but she didn't react to it just then. Maybe getting out of the area would ease it, if they could just make it that far.

A cold wind hit her full in the face as she opened the back door of the Jeep for Kai. Three days until Christmas Eve, she realized, and they were no closer to solving this case. Yes, Poppy had given her the name of the man who had sold the drugs to her friends, but whether that would lead them anywhere productive, she couldn't be sure.

As soon as they were ensconced in the Jeep, Bridger wanted to know what she had learned.

"Poppy said a man by the name of Tripp Hughes sells the drugs to her friends. But many of the locals have been angry because youth at local colleges have been turning up dead because they have taken drugs found to be laced with fentanyl without their knowledge. They believe those drugs have all come from Hughes, whether directly or indirectly." Sophie paused, watching a young man hunkered in only a hoodie cross the street. His face could easily be described as gaunt and his form was far too skinny. But there had been something about him that attracted Sophie's notice.

"Does he look familiar?" Sophie asked. But the guy had ducked his head into his hoodie before she could get the words out.

"Not sure. I didn't really get a good look at his face." Bridger leaned over to look in the rearview mirror as they drove past.

"Probably my imagination. Anyway, Poppy said one of her friends asked Hughes if he was giving them bad drugs and he got angry with him and never really answered. But aside from all that, she told me she wants to get clean. She said Sarah had talked to her about how she had just recently quit drugs and was going through a recovery program. But then she had heard Sarah and this Hughes guy had had words a few nights before Sarah was found dead." Sophie looked into the back seat to find Kai already napping.

"That sounds pretty suspicious to me. So, where do Tripp Hughes and this Rocky fella fit together?" Bridger gripped the wheel as a light in front of them turned and they had to stop again.

"I don't know. Poppy said she had heard of Rocky, of course, but didn't really know which one he was. I'm still trying to figure out exactly what that meant. I didn't want to interrupt her to ask." Sophie's brow creased.

"I get the feeling this Rocky guy and some of his friends might have been pedaling more than drugs." Bridger pressed his lips together in an expression Sophie was coming to recognize as anger.

"Do you mean like prostitution or something?" Sophie hated to ask, but she needed to know.

"Yes, exactly. He didn't seem to approach any of the younger girls, but the ones he knew to be at least of age… I sure hope I'm wrong, though." Bridger watched a white, beat-up, nineties-model truck creep across the intersection in front of them as he spoke.

"Oh, I see." Sophie shuddered, turning the heater in the Jeep up higher. She was ready to get out of this area of town. It was hard to tell if her shivering was due to the cold or the apprehension their surroundings incited.

She was glad they were headed back to Bridger's ranch.

That afternoon, Sophie and Kai accompanied Bridger to his office to do some digging on Tripp Hughes and any connections they could find by the name of Rocky. Pulling some files, they soon learned Tripp Hughes had had several prior arrests, but nothing that had kept him in prison for long. They did find a current address, so Bridger wanted to try for an impromptu questioning.

"I don't think he's our guy, but maybe he can answer some questions that will lead us to the killer." Bridger tapped his lips with his index finger. "Let's have Campbell go with us. He can help keep watch."

It surprised Sophie that Bridger wanted her to go along, but she supposed he wanted to keep her close considering all that had happened. When his brother arrived, they loaded Kai in the Jeep. Campbell would follow in his patrol unit. Putting the street name Lydia had given them into a maps app, Bridger paused in surprise.

"What is it?" Sophie asked, noticing his silence.

"This isn't far from the tornado site where Agent Benton was found." Bridger puzzled over it a moment longer, zooming in and out to look at the street names.

"What do you think the connection is?" Sophie leaned in to look at his screen. It had to be the area Lydia had described, and she even knew it was at the end of a cul-de-sac. She'd said she had been there a few times with Carter, but never paid attention to the address number.

"I don't know. Maybe nothing." Bridger squinted at the phone a little longer before slipping it back into his pocket. "Let's just hope the house and Hughes are both still there."

When they reached the cul-de-sac on the street the girl had described, the house was indeed still standing. Noting the address for future reference, Bridger cautiously led the approach to the front door. But after several attempts, he gave up on getting an answer to his knocking.

Bridger frowned and shook his head.

"I don't buy it. Go sit with Campbell. I'm going to try to get around back to take a good look. He's probably not the kind of guy to just answer the door for anyone who knocks." He glanced up, noting a security camera peering at him from the corner of the doorway. He pulled his SIG from his waistband then, providing Sophie all the prompting she needed to get out of sight.

Bridger started around the side of the house and Sophie moved toward Campbell's patrol unit. She had only gone a few steps, however, when Campbell threw open his door with a shout of warning, gun drawn.

It was too late. Sophie let out a shriek just before a hand clamped around her neck and over her mouth.

The sound of the hammer clicking as the nose of the pistol connected with her temple silenced any questions as her blood nearly froze in her veins.

THIRTEEN

Bridger whirled to find the man holding Sophie in a death grip under the Glock in his hand. Bridger's heart nearly seized in his chest at the sight of Sophie's eyes, wide and full and terror-filled. Sophie's attacker kicked Kai away as the dog growled at him in warning.

"Drop your weapons." The gunman, dark hood over his head and a ski mask covering his face, was already dragging Sophie away. Bridger lowered the SIG as Campbell lowered his Smith & Wesson on the other side.

Sophie stumbled, eyes pleading with Bridger to help her. Kai kept her distance for the moment but continued to growl low in her throat, a warning that she wasn't giving up. It only served to irritate Sophie's assailant, though.

"Make it shut up!" He lashed out at the dog again, nearly losing his grip on Sophie. But as she tried to take advantage of it, he jerked her up even harder, squeezing her head tight against his chest.

Bridger had his hands up. "She can't give the order to the dog with your hand over her mouth."

"You tell it, then." Sophie's assailant jerked his chin upward for emphasis. Bridger did as the man said, but Kai was only silenced for a moment.

With an angry yell at Kai to shut up, Sophie's attacker

dragged her toward the house. Kai followed, now dodging in and out at his ankles, forward and back on her haunches in a sort of dance, narrowly avoiding the man's lashing feet where he continued to kick at her. The struggle was beginning to become too much for Sophie's attacker though and he was losing his cool.

"Call it off." He did the unthinkable then and swung the nose of his Glock toward Kai.

"Kai, cease!" Bridger could only hope the dog would obey.

Infuriated by his threats against her furry best friend, however, Sophie retaliated in a single ferocious burst of energy. In one swift motion, she became a frenzy of arms and legs as her attacker let out a yelp of pain. While her assailant jerked his hand from her mouth, she swung out at his weapon, knocking the Glock loose from his hand as it went off with a crack. She had aimed well, though, sending the nose of the gun up into the air just in time as Kai lunged in to help her. The Glock clattered to the ground near the curb and Sophie kicked it away as Kai grasped the man's dark pant leg.

Bridger and Campbell reacted quickly, as well, both grabbing their guns in what seemed only a millisecond, aiming them at Sophie's attacker as she slipped out of the way, calling Kai off with her as she went.

Relief flooded Bridger as Sophie and Kai slid behind him and Campbell moved in to cuff the man. Campbell read him his rights while urging him toward his patrol unit.

Bridger held up a hand to ask Campbell to pause, however, and took the hood and mask from the man's head. "Are you Tripp Hughes?"

"I ain't answerin' none of your questions. I want a lawyer." The gunman's weak blue eyes, red around the rims and watery, shot venom in their direction as he glared from Bridger to Sophie and back again.

But that pretty well answered Bridger's question. And not only was the guy Hughes, but the man knew exactly who Bridger and Sophie were as well. Why else would he have attacked Sophie?

He might not be the killer, but Bridger felt certain this guy was in cahoots with the man who was. He was younger than Bridger had expected, though. Whoever ran this operation sure seemed to be targeting a lot of young people.

Bridger's phone rang while Campbell was settling Hughes into the patrol unit. "Detective Cole."

A hesitation on the other end of the line came at first. Then a quiet female voice spoke. "Poppy Flynn is missing."

"Lydia?" Bridger sent a look of concern toward Sophie. "How long has she been missing?"

Lydia kept her voice low on the other end, as if afraid of being overheard. "No one has seen or heard from her since the memorial service this morning."

It was growing dark out and the winter air settled around them like a layer of ice between gusts of wind. It was no time for anyone to be out in the elements.

"Listen to me, Lydia. I need you to gather up everyone you can who's willing to help look for Poppy. Meet us at the community center in half an hour. We need to find her ASAP." Bridger waited for her confirmation before disconnecting.

He turned to find Sophie looking at him expectantly. "It's Poppy." Bridger relayed the information he had just learned from Lydia. "Do you think Kai can find her?"

"If we can narrow it down, probably so. We can start at the community center since she was there this morning. But it would really help if we had something with Poppy's scent on it. Kai is trained to air scent, but she needs to know who she's trying to find in this case. Just trying to locate a random person would be difficult for her. She needs to know what scent she's looking for to be able to make it work." Sophie's eyes were filled with emotion.

"We'll do our best to come up with something." Bridger put a reassuring hand on her arm.

"I feel like I've put her in danger by talking to her." Sophie shook her head. "How did Lydia know?"

"This isn't your fault, Sophie. She chose to talk to you. And I'm not sure who, but I'm pretty positive someone was watching us the entire time we were at the community center. To be honest, I think many of these kids were already in danger before we ever showed up." Bridger motioned to her Jeep. "Get Kai loaded up while I tell Campbell what's going on. He can get a search party together. Lydia's gathering up some of their friends to help as well."

But when they arrived at the community center, only Lydia and a couple of other young women waited for them. "Is this it or are we waiting for some others?" Bridger's demeanor had switched into professional mode, and Lydia shrank back. He would have to remember to soften his tone a bit.

"This is it. Everyone's afraid to try to help a cop." Lydia spat the last word out as though she had somehow learned the word represented something terrible.

Bridger tried not to take offense. "Okay, I get that. We have Kai at least, and a search party will be organized soon. We could use something to get Poppy's scent from, though."

The girls looked at each other and shrugged, no one offering up any assistance or information.

Sophie stepped forward. "Do any of you know where Poppy lives?"

Again the girls exchanged glances. Finally, Lydia spoke up. "She lives with her parents. They don't know she's missing yet, though. She was supposed to be with Nova. But she's not answering any of our text messages."

"And have any of you tried calling her?" Bridger tried again.

They all looked at him like he was an alien with two heads.

"No, of course not." Lydia seemed to be the spokesperson. "She wouldn't answer anyway."

As if that explained it all. Teenagers definitely had some different ideas.

"I suggest we make sure she isn't safe at home before we all go off looking for her. Maybe she got her phone taken away or something." Bridger was about to call Campbell and tell him to call off the search party when another girl finally spoke.

"She's not at home. We found her car and it isn't at her house. It's trashed." The dark-haired young woman had tears sparkling in her brown eyes. Bridger hadn't even thought Poppy was old enough to drive.

"I feel like there's something you ladies aren't telling us." Sophie frowned at them all one by one, hands on her hips. The three sets of eyes she tried to look into all suddenly found their toes and fixated on them.

"Lorenzo said that he overheard Rocky on the phone. He said something about making Poppy pay. I think they knew she talked to you this morning." It was Lydia speaking once more.

"And how would he know? How did you know?" Sophie looked at each face again before settling on Lydia with raised brows. She had no idea who Lorenzo was, but she assumed they believed him. Then Lydia confirmed Bridger's suspicions.

"Because someone was spying on her."

Sophie's heart pounded in anxiety. Maybe they hadn't been watching Sophie and Bridger as much as Poppy? Either way, it wasn't good. What would these people do to the girl for talking to them? Did they know what Poppy had told them?

Could she and Bridger find her in time?

"We need her home address, ASAP. And then you all need to go home and lay low. You took a risk here, and I appreciate it, but I don't want you winding up missing as well." Bridger braced his fists on his hips.

"They won't touch any of us. Nova's boyfriend has a lot of influence." This came from the third girl who hadn't spoken yet. "But Rocky doesn't like Poppy. Doesn't trust her. Says her family is too goody-goody."

Sophie didn't think she wanted to analyze that statement too much. Lydia kept her from having to do so when she spoke again. "Yeah, Lexie's right. And they didn't like how close Poppy was to Sarah. I think someone was watching Sarah, too. But we aren't going home until we know Poppy is safe. We don't want her to end up like Sarah. Or Bailey."

"Fine, we can meet you back here after we meet with her family, but they need to know Poppy is missing." Bridger waited until Lydia gave him the address and thanked them.

In less than five minutes, they were headed to Poppy's address—a middle-class home in a suburban neighborhood. It wasn't what Sophie would have expected, considering the part of town they had found her in.

Bridger had briefly asked for more details about who was spying on Poppy and why before leaving, but he'd received only shrugs and noncommittal replies. He'd decided it was a waste of valuable time—time they didn't have if they wanted to find Poppy safe.

He knocked on the door of a modest two-story home, which was answered shortly by a pretty blond lady who resembled an older version of Poppy.

"May I help you?" She smiled, looking from one to the other.

"We'd like to talk to you for a moment about Poppy." Bridger showed the woman his badge. "Are you her mother?"

She placed a hand to her mouth. "Yes. I'm Emily Flynn. Please tell me that child is not in trouble."

Bridger hesitated only briefly. "We hope not. She's missing."

The woman stepped back and motioned them in, a shocked expression clouding her face.

"Oh, my." Emily lowered herself to the sofa but then bounded right back up. "You're sure? She's not with those hoodlum friends of hers?"

"Her friends sent us, actually." Bridger ignored Emily's assessment of Poppy's friends.

This revelation seemed to spur Emily into action. "Oh, Poppy. We have to find her. I'll get my purse. Her father's at the office, but I'll call him on the way."

"Wait!" Sophie broke in. "This is my search and rescue dog, Kai. Do you have anything belonging to Poppy that she's recently worn? It'll help Kai to find your daughter."

Emily looked at Kai as if only just seeing her for the first time. "Oh. Oh, yes. Let me get something."

When Emily returned a moment later with a red sweater in her hands, her eyes were filled with tears. She handed the sweater to Sophie. "She wore this last night to a Christmas party we attended with her father's business. Please tell me we'll find her. I can't bear to face Christmas without my little girl."

Sophie's heart broke for the woman. She had to fight back tears of her own as Bridger replied as honestly as he could.

"We're going to do everything we can, Mrs. Flynn."

Bridger gave Emily the address to the community center where they would begin their search. "I think it's best if you take your own vehicle. We may need to go in different directions."

He had already sent Campbell to watch over Lydia and her friends. He had made them promise to wait there until he and Sophie could return to the community center, but he didn't want anything to happen to the girls.

A small group of officers and search teams had gathered at the center by the time they returned, and Sophie wasted no time in setting Kai to work. Allowing her a good sniff of the sweater, she gave the dog the command to search. It reassured Sophie to see Kai doing what she was trained to do and knowing they were doing everything they could to find Poppy quickly.

Emily Flynn had arrived just after they had, introducing her husband, Gary, as they came in. He had apparently driven over to meet her there.

Bridger stayed with Sophie and Kai while Campbell organized the rest of the search efforts.

Bridger and Sophie followed Kai's nose on a haphazard path at first, but she soon appeared to pick up a definite trail. The canine followed it until she reached a small parking lot. Then she paused and raised her head, looking off into the darkness.

"Kai lost the scent. Poppy probably got into a vehicle

here. This could take some time." Sophie gave Bridger an apologetic look. "I'd hoped wherever she had been taken it was on foot. That wasn't realistic, of course."

Bridger nodded and made a gesture toward Kai. "It's okay. Let her work."

"We could use something more to go on. If they traveled very far by car, she probably won't be able to pick up Poppy's scent again from here." Sophie studied the ground and then the parking lot around them. Kai kept sniffing the ground around her, raising her nose into the air again as Sophie spoke. "If we can at least get an idea of which direction the vehicle went, maybe it'll move us in the right direction."

Bridger bent down to study some dirt in the crevices of the asphalt but then shook his head. "There isn't enough dirt accumulated here to see the tire marks clearly. We need to ask Lydia and her friends a few more questions. Maybe she took her car from here to somewhere else. They said they found her car. If we can find it, maybe we can go from there."

Sophie nodded, giving Kai a command that allowed her to relax her search momentarily. As they trudged back to the center, Sophie spoke kindly to Kai to ease the dog's anxiety. Kai's posture—lowered head and drooping ears—told Sophie that Kai was disappointed at being called off the search without succeeding at finding her person. She didn't perk up again until Sophie explained that they weren't finished yet, only taking a break to regroup.

"It's like she understands every word you're saying." Bridger shook his head in amazement, admiration for the dog apparent in his turquoise eyes.

"I believe she does." Sophie gave Kai a loving pat and

smiled at Bridger. "And she loves to do her job. But she wants to be successful."

After speaking to Lydia and her friends once again, Sophie and Bridger learned the approximate location of Poppy's car, got a description of it, and lit out to find it and resume their search for Poppy.

Five minutes across town, they found Poppy's little red convertible Beetle in the parking lot across from the coffee shop that one of the young women had said she often frequented, just where she had last seen it. As she had said, someone had done some significant damage to the car. The front windshield was smashed, one of the tires was slashed, and scratches ran down one side of the car from the front bumper to the back fender.

"Yikes, it looks like someone was pretty angry about her talking to us all right." Sophie winced at the sight of the little car.

"I'd say someone was sending a message about something, for sure." Bridger pulled out his phone to send a text. "I'll see if there are any prints here, but I doubt whoever did this touched anything with their hands. It looks like they used a tire iron."

"Ugh. What a jerk." Sophie was already presenting the sweater to Kai again, and the dog barely sniffed it before trotting off after Poppy's scent. Sophie's hopes soared as she took it up so quickly.

But they had only followed her for a few minutes when those hopes were dashed again. After Kai led them in and out of corners and alleys, she slowed as she reached another area of the street that looked like someone had recently been parked there. A dribble of oil settled into a puddle between some faint white parking markers and Kai stopped and whined dolefully. She was frustrated as well.

"Whoever took her put her into another vehicle here and left with her?" Bridger spoke Sophie's fears aloud in the form of a question.

"It looks that way." Sophie frowned.

Cold seeped into the threads of her clothing, the chilly wind turning her nose icy and her fingers numb beneath her gloves. But concern for Poppy outweighed her discomfort and she pressed on. The young woman hadn't been dressed warmly that morning, from what Sophie could remember. Hopefully, she had changed or found a coat in her car at least.

Twinkling lights from the neighborhood just beyond the main street reminded her, too, that Christmas was inching ever closer. They all certainly wanted this finished in time to be back home with their families, gathered over a hot meal with the homey scents of a crackling fire intermingling with pumpkin pie and spiced cider accompanied by the happy Christmas carols and smiles from loved ones. A wave of nostalgia hit Sophie a little too hard and an ache pierced her stomach. They had to finish this, and quickly.

Bridger was studying her closely and she felt herself flush under his scrutiny, knowing he had noticed the sparkle of tears gathering in her eyes, even in the dim light from the streetlamps.

"We'll find her. And she's going to be okay." He grasped her gloved hand in his and the warmth of his touch made her long for impossible things. She could see herself leaning on this handsome, dependable cowboy for the rest of her life.

Headlights appeared in the quiet street then, coming toward them.

"It's a county unit. Maybe Campbell." Bridger released Sophie's hand.

When the SUV stopped beside them and the window

rolled down, Campbell was indeed the driver. "We got a tip that she might have been taken out of town. Why don't you guys go home and get some rest tonight and we'll see what we can come up with by morning. It's too dark and cold to be out looking all night. Those friends seem to think she's safe for the moment."

Sophie's stomach turned over. What else were those girls not telling them?

"What do you mean by that?" Bridger gave Sophie a suspicious look as well.

Campbell sighed. "I'm not sure I trust them. They've all of a sudden started saying they might have made a mistake. The taller one that does all the talking says some of their guy friends think Poppy was secretly seeing one of their friends. Now the story is that she might have just run off with him."

Sophie stiffened. "But that doesn't make sense. Why would her car have been all beat up if she simply ran off with some guy?"

Campbell looked over at Sophie, eyes very much like Bridger's, and shrugged. "They said another one of the guys was jealous because he'd been asking her out and she refused. They think he saw her leaving with the other fella, caught on, and decided to get revenge on her by smashing up her car. I don't know if it's true or if they are just making it all up as they go along. I personally think they're up to something."

Bridger nodded slowly. "I think you're right. And I think whatever it is, none of them are on our side."

FOURTEEN

Bridger watched Sophie's face fall as realization set in. He knew she was probably feeling naïve and foolish, because he'd felt that way himself earlier when he'd begun to suspect something just like his brother had suggested. When he and Sophie were asking the girls about Poppy's car, there had been something suspicious in their manner. He hadn't been able to quite put his finger on it at the time, but as they searched for Poppy throughout the evening, he had started to wonder if the girls were actually trustworthy.

"You think they're lying to us?" Sophie asked.

"I can't be sure, but I do think they know more than they're telling us." Bridger chose his words carefully. He thought someone might be feeding the girls their dialog, so to speak. Someone was telling them exactly what to say to him and Sophie, and his brother as well, if he wasn't mistaken, and he could only wonder if they were doing it under coercion or of their own accord.

Sophie had a hand to her mouth. "So do you think Poppy's in on it, too? Or do you think they're just using her? Whoever it is…"

"I don't know that, either, but it's too big of a risk to take not to try to find her. Let's chat a little more with her mother and see what we can learn." Bridger motioned toward the

Jeep. He had noticed her teeth chattering for a little while now. It was past time for her to take a break and warm up. He would welcome the opportunity, as well, honestly.

Emily Flynn had given Campbell her contact information, so when he called her, she reluctantly agreed to meet them to answer a few more questions. This time Bridger suggested his office. If he was right about the girls, there could be someone listening to everything that went on at the community center.

After a long question-and-answer session with Poppy's mother, Bridger was about to give up on learning anything useful. "Mrs. Flynn, could you request phone records for Poppy's number? I could subpoena them, but it would be much faster for you to simply request them, since it would require a warrant. And we don't have time to waste."

Emily Flynn's eyes widened then and she sat up a little straighter. "Her phone!"

Bridger didn't get too hopeful. Tracking the phone would be too easy. No doubt, Poppy's captors had taken care of that little detail by now, either removing the battery or destroying it. "What about her phone?"

"It's linked to her iPad. We could access her messages with it. We can get them much more quickly that way." Emily rose to her feet. "It's at home in her room. I can get it in just a few minutes."

Sophie's expression reflected his own mixed feelings—encouraged but cautious. And growing weary. Bridger gave her a nod.

"Okay, but make it fast. We need to get back to looking for her." Bridger wanted this over, but he knew the Flynns did, too. And he sincerely hoped finding Poppy would bring them closer to finding Agent Benton's killer and whoever was after Sophie.

* * *

The iPad took a bit of time to go through, but they found very little of any relevance. If Poppy truly had a secret boyfriend, she hadn't left any evidence of communicating with him via text. Of course, there was always the possibility of other apps like Snapchat where the messages were deleted after they were read. But there was nothing suspicious on Poppy's phone that Bridger could see. They also went through all her social media accounts but found no pictures or messages that gave them any clue of who might have taken her or where she might be. But it also didn't confirm what Lydia had told them.

He called Campbell then. "Send Lydia and her friends home. Let them think we believe their story and let's see where they go and who they talk to."

Kai and Sophie were both as restless as Bridger was, and Emily Flynn paced, checking her phone every few minutes for a message from her husband, who was still out searching for Poppy.

The minutes ticked by slowly, and Bridger finally gave up on the iPad he had been going through and told Mrs. Flynn to go home as well. Apparently, she'd instead gone back to looking for her daughter, even though Bridger had implored her to let them do the searching. He couldn't really blame her, though, if he were honest about it. He could see Poppy's parents really loved her. They just hadn't been able to moderate her choices well in the past few months, it seemed. Teenaged willfulness scared him all the way to his toes. Kids seemed to have no idea of the dangers they put themselves in so readily.

Campbell called back over forty-five minutes later. "Looks like a small party going on in a run-down house outside of town. Might be worth checking out. If the supposedly missing girl is involved in whatever they're trying to pull, she might be there."

Bridger got the address and thanked his brother. Sophie waited patiently while Bridger caught her up on Campbell's news as they drove. "We'll have to be invisible observers until we can determine if she's there or not. If she is, we'll bring in a team."

They parked a good distance from the old farmhouse and walked the final yards to the address, keeping to the shadows away from the two-lane road. Before they reached a good vantage point to peek into the house, though, someone came out, talking on the phone in an angry voice.

"I don't care. Keep her in the warehouse. If that cop and his girlfriend come around, be ready. You can't move her right now." He paused for only a moment. "It isn't going to happen. He wants the cops to get them there in the morning. Not before. Have your men cause another distraction or something but stick with the rest of the plan."

Bridger grasped Sophie's upper arm, and when she looked at him, he could read the conflicted emotions in her eyes. Gesturing toward where they had parked the Jeep, he motioned they should go back.

"You can't think she's in that same warehouse that burned." Sophie spoke in a whisper as soon as they were out of hearing range, even though the door had closed on the man long before they had traveled this far.

"She's either there or she's here and we've been set up again. But I want you and Kai to wait in the Jeep, with the doors locked, until I can make sure she isn't here." Bridger put her in the Jeep and locked the doors. "I mean it. Here are the keys. If I'm not back in ten minutes, head back to town and find my brother."

Bridger hoped he was doing the right thing. But something told him he needed to see inside the farmhouse before leaving.

Sophie wanted nothing more than to find Poppy and go home.

Weary of all the games, she coaxed Kai's head into her lap and stroked her soft fur lovingly. Bridger seemed energized by the hunt for the missing young woman, but Sophie didn't share his enthusiasm. She closed her eyes for a moment just to let some of the anxious thoughts float away.

She had never considered her work on a SAR team would lead her here. She didn't regret it, but she wouldn't miss the danger following her around when this was over. She had lived a pretty quiet life until recently.

Thoughts of how different Bridger's life must be from hers reminded her that he wouldn't be in her life much longer. It almost frightened her how easily he had come to be a comfortable part of her everyday existence, and it frightened her how much the idea of him missing from her daily life made her chest ache. Just the thought filled her with emptiness. And that was an emotion she tried to avoid at all costs. She had felt so empty after losing her husband Troy that she had wondered for a while if she would ever be whole again in this life. Gradually, she had begun to fill the void after beginning training with Kai, and she did her best to fill the rest of her time with work and making up for lost time with her mother. Bridger had not only filled the hollowness lately but made her hopeful again.

She had known better than to allow herself to have feelings for him.

But if she were honest, she hadn't really had control of the matter. He was everything good and kind, and she was drawn to him irresistibly. The impossibility of a relationship between them was irrelevant.

A few minutes later, Bridger's broad shoulders appeared in the shadowy night, striding back toward her purposefully, and she released a breath she hadn't realized she'd been holding. His cowboy hat cast him in a larger-than-life silhouette like a hero in an old Western movie, and her heart leapt with happiness at the sight of him.

Oh, boy, was she in trouble.

"I don't think Poppy's inside. I couldn't see her anywhere and none of their actions gave any indication that she was being held anywhere. No guards, no one watching doors or windows, nothing out of the ordinary for a bunch of kids having a party." Bridger rubbed his hands together after closing the door.

"So we're headed back to the warehouse?" Sophie already knew the answer, though.

"If she isn't there, we're going home for the night." Bridger gave her a look that discouraged any argument.

Sophie nodded and settled in for the ride. Either he was confident Poppy was there or he was finished playing games tonight, too. Whichever it was, Sophie wasn't about to argue right now. Fatigue had settled around her long ago and she wasn't sure they were getting anywhere just now anyway.

Before driving away, Bridger picked up his phone. "I'm going to let Campbell know where we're headed."

They drove in relative silence back into town. The warehouse, though burned out now, was still standing in several places. It had caution tape strung all the way around it, along with warning signs to keep out, but some sort of dim light flickered in a small window on a corner of the structure that still stood. The walls there were practically untouched, and the lingering scent of smoke didn't completely conceal the scent of a new fire as they drew closer on foot. However, it appeared this one had been built for warmth instead of destruction. It was flickering harmlessly in the windows, and peering in through the smudged glass, Bridger could see that someone had built a makeshift fire pit around the logs to keep it contained. They were using the fire for both illumination and a heat source.

Kai whined and fidgeted on her leash. "Poppy's here. Kai's caught her scent." Sophie whispered the words before giving Kai a quiet command.

"Keep her on her leash just in case." Bridger put out a hand to stay them both as he leaned closer in an attempt to get a better look.

After several seconds passed, he eased back toward them, careful to make very little noise. "It looks like she's alone, but I'm not sure I'm buying it."

"Me, either." Sophie wrapped her free arm around her. "What now?"

"We're going to get her before they know we're here." Bridger had taken off his cowboy hat, and his thick, wavy hair stood up as a cold wind filtered through the alley.

The cold air wasn't the only thing that made Sophie shiver. "Are you sure this is a good idea?"

"I think we have to act now. The man we overheard on the phone at the party said they wanted us to show up in the morning. If we get to her now, we have the element of surprise on our side." He was already drawing his SIG.

"And how do we know Poppy isn't on their side, working against us, like the other girls?" Sophie hated to admit it, but the possibility stung. She had liked Poppy and wanted to help her.

"It's a chance we have to take." Bridger's words didn't reassure her.

With a nod of resolve, she let out a breath. "Tell me what to do."

"If it's clear, I'm going to send you after Poppy while I stay on guard. I'll make sure it's safe before letting you leave my side." His eyes darkened with something for a moment and she thought she glimpsed a flicker of fear before his expression turned neutral again. "I'm sorry you're having to go through all this, Sophie."

She wasn't sure if he was referring to saving Poppy or just all of it, including being chased by a killer, but either way she accepted his words with a lump in her throat. "I'm just glad I have you to help me through it."

He stared at her for a moment, expression inscrutable, before nodding. "Let's go."

Sophie gave Kai a command that would keep her silent to prevent her from alerting anyone they hadn't yet seen to their presence. She grasped her leash with quaking hands before following Bridger into the darkness.

This time they entered through a scorched wall of the warehouse, Bridger checking carefully to be sure that the structure was stable the whole way in. Even over twenty-four hours later, the lingering acrid smell of smoke still stung her nose. Some of the chemical smell was gone, but the odor reminded her of destruction and loss and she pushed back another wave of emotion. The last few days had been a roller coaster of adrenaline and excitement, for good or bad, and the effects drained her. But Poppy had seemed utterly sincere and she wouldn't abandon the girl to the hands of the monsters they were up against.

Creeping closer to the corner room that remained unconsumed by the flames, Bridger checked every shadowy space for danger before allowing Sophie passage. Finally, they were there, and he tried the door. It was locked, but he had come prepared. Taking out a small tool, he worked carefully for a few seconds before a click allowed the handle to turn. Bridger took one last good look around before slipping inside.

Sophie followed and was about to rush over to Poppy's side to release her when the girl's muffled voice beneath a gag tried to warn her of what was coming.

A dark leather glove shot out to grab Sophie by the neck just as another shadow lunged at Bridger. Her breath caught suddenly. Kai jerked against her leash and let out a fierce bark just as Sophie let it go.

FIFTEEN

Bridger saw Sophie practically fling the end of Kai's leash just before the punch struck his jaw with a jarring impact. He shook his head, but before he could fully recover, a second man grabbed him. Kai stood in the middle of them all, growling, not sure where to begin.

"Nice of you to join us." A deep voice sounded from behind her. "You wouldn't just die quietly, so it's time we have a little talk."

Bridger groaned, realizing the men had been waiting in the room on the second story just above them, the unnatural openings in the building allowing them both a good place to hide and easy access to the floor below. He had heard them slipping down to the ground floor just a second too late.

"Tripp, get the dog. I believe you're familiar with it." The same deep voice, and even more casual amusement, flooded his tone this time. "Go on. Face your fears and all that."

The man, apparently already released on bond, looked insulted at the order, but he followed it anyway, jerking up Kai's leash and dragging her away.

A wordless grunt of protest came from Poppy's gagged mouth, but Sophie remained silent, knowing it wouldn't help anything at this moment. She wanted to thrash away from the man holding her and go after her sweet girl, but it was impossible with the five men surrounding them. One stood over Poppy now, also, and two still stood holding Bridger. It gave her a small amount of satisfaction to know it took two of them to hold him, though it did little good right now.

"Now then. We need to know who you're working for, and what you know. Tie their hands and feet." The man with the deep voice cocked a gun, put it to her head and walked around to stand between them. He held it at her forehead and Sophie had the sudden terrifying thought that this was Agent Benton's killer. His face, however, was shrouded in a ski mask, unlike the other men, which she found strange. Why would he remain so determined to conceal his identity if, as she suspected, he planned to kill them eventually anyway?

His attention settled on Bridger, despite the gun to Sophie's head. "Come on, now. I have three hostages here. There's no way you're getting out of this."

"Detective Bridger Cole, Texas Rangers. She's an innocent bystander who just happened to be working with search and rescue teams after the tornado where the body was found. She's no danger to you." Bridger strained against the men holding him, not really trying to get loose, but not letting their job remain too easy, either. It wouldn't hurt anything to tire them out.

"Texas Ranger. What a hero. Too bad you lost this one." Deep Voice snickered. "And whether or not she's a danger is up for discussion. I need to know what she saw."

Bridger wasn't sure how to respond to this. Finally, he settled on telling him what he knew. "She saw a woman's body in the debris of the tornado. The woman had a gunshot wound to the head, making it obvious her death was not caused by the storm. She reported her findings and showed me where the body was located."

"And?" He sounded impatient. "What else did she see?"

"That's it. Someone started shooting at us when we returned to the victim. Later we collected what evidence we could and left. Nothing significant, unfortunately."

He looked at Sophie then. "Is he telling the truth? Is that really all you saw?"

She nodded. "What else was there to see?"

The slender man just stared at her through the eyeholes of his mask, as if assessing her honesty or trying to make her squirm. Bridger silently willed her to remain calm. He wished he could communicate with her. They needed to keep these guys talking until help could get there. He just prayed Stetson or Campbell would arrange backup and arrive soon, but he had no idea how long it would be until they realized he needed help.

"You were suspicious of her, weren't you?" Bridger asked the question this time. "The woman. You knew her, but you didn't trust her."

Deep Voice turned to look at Bridger again. "What do you know about that?"

Bridger shrugged slowly, trying to gauge if the man really knew who Sarah was. "I know she was shot right in the middle of the forehead, the way you're holding the gun to her head now. And the girl found dead in the warehouse was shot the same way." He hesitated to use Sophie's name in case this man didn't know who she was. Bridger wouldn't give the guy any ammunition.

"That isn't that unusual. Go on." The man jerked the pistol at Sophie's forehead, as if reminding him who was in charge.

"Rumor has it she was talking to some of your addicts

about getting clean. I don't think you wanted that. Was she selling for you, or just hanging out and influencing your other dealers?" Bridger was careful to leave out names.

"What difference does it make? She shouldn't have been hanging around. She got in over her head and tried to take some of my associates out with her. I couldn't have that." He shifted his stance. "Which of those kids has been talking?"

Bridger winced internally, but he was careful to keep an inscrutable expression. He had hoped the guy wouldn't ask that. "I can't remember names. Besides, they knew I was a cop and I doubt they even used their real names."

"This one did, didn't she?" He jerked a head toward Poppy. "Did she tell you her name?"

Bridger stood silent for a moment. "I believe her friends told us her name was Poppy when she came up missing."

"Don't play games with me. I know you talked to Poppy at the center yesterday. What did she tell you?" His tone turned harsh.

"She talked to my friend here, not me. I believe all she told her was that she was friends with Sarah and that Sarah had talked to her about rehab." Bridger continued to choose his words carefully. "The next thing we knew, she was missing."

A grunt, which was left open to interpretation, was all he got from the man. So he asked another question of his own. "Did you put those other girls up to feeding us information?"

Just a shrug. "Maybe. Again, it doesn't matter. You can't trust anyone these days, you know. I thought a cop would know that."

Bridger wanted to deny the validity of his statement, but he had learned the hard way to be careful whom he trusted. And apparently, he was still learning.

"You're pretty young for a Texas Ranger, aren't you? I thought the Rangers were pretty much all old guys." The man laughed at his own words. Bridger didn't find it to be much of a joke. It did confirm his suspicions, however, that this guy was young himself, despite the position of power he seemed to hold over the others.

"Most of the guys are a little older than me, but I wouldn't call them old. I respect the other men a great deal. It takes time to get good experience." Bridger didn't care what this degenerate thought. It did make him wonder just how old he was beneath the mask, however. He had the build of a young man, for sure, but Bridger had seen many drug addicts waste away to almost nothing because of their addiction.

Sophie was listening in silence, but he noticed she kept watching Kai, who still let out a growl on occasion, even though Hughes jerked on her leash with unnecessary vigor every time she did. He still kept a good distance from Kai, though, as if terrified to even be in the same room with her.

Bridger didn't know how long he could keep this guy talking. He had laughed at his words about the other Rangers, though Bridger wasn't sure what he found so amusing about what Bridger had said. It struck him odd that the man knew anything about the Rangers, anyway, but he filed the thought away. Maybe he had somehow had a run-in with the Rangers before, though the idea surprised Bridger. It probably wouldn't have turned out well if he had.

"Were you also suspicious of the girl at the warehouse? Is that why you shot her?" Bridger tried for a little more time and information.

"Hey, I'm not admitting to shooting anyone. If the girl was killed, there was a good reason. Maybe she stuck her nose into other people's business. Maybe she didn't pay her debts. Who can say? It's a tough world these days." He looked at Sophie again. "Right, dog lover? You sure you don't have anything else to tell me? You've been too quiet."

In a sudden motion, he turned the gun on Bridger. "Maybe I should shoot your boyfriend. He doesn't want to offer up any good information, anyway."

Bridger winced as Sophie shrieked. "Don't, please!"

She squeezed her eyes closed.

"What do you know?" The man stepped closer to Bridger, motioning for one of the men holding him to take hold of Sophie.

"I don't know any more than what he's told you. I saw the woman's body, went for help, and someone's been trying to kill me ever since." Sophie was shaking her head furiously.

Bridger prayed she would stay calm.

"You sure?" He put the gun to Bridger's head and an ominous click echoed through the smoky room. A small window provided the only ventilation besides the slightly open door and Bridger had to fight the urge to cough. If he did, the guy might react by shooting him.

"I'm sure. I didn't see anything more." Sophie's chin went up a notch, though the fear didn't leave her eyes.

Bridger was holding his breath. What would this reckless man do? How desperate was he?

The Glock shook slightly against his forehead and Bridger silently prayed for help and guidance. Sophie needed him.

His answer came in the sound of feet dropping from the floor above just outside the door.

It was apparently their lookout. He came in shouting. "Boss, we got trouble. More cops coming. Lots of them."

The man holding the gun on Bridger dropped it to his side and fled as if the place had exploded. Behind him, the other men darted away, as well, each heading for any possible exit in a rush to get away before they could be arrested.

"Hughes, get rid of them." The shout came from the fleeing man in the mask.

Tripp Hughes, however, had already scurried out ahead of some of the others. An argument ensued as he called the order back to one of the other men.

"I'm not getting their blood on my hands. I'm not a cop killer." The guy Hughes had called to, by the name of Bourke, shook his head as he continued to bolt.

Resigned, Hughes returned to stand in front of Bridger first. He yanked a gun from his back waistband and Sophie screamed as he leveled it at Bridger's temple.

She squeezed her eyes closed and lunged toward Hughes but, before she could reach him, he crumpled to the ground in a heap.

Looking around, she realized one of the officers who had come to their aid stood on the opposite remaining wall with a long-range rifle in his hand. He gave her a nod as he jumped down to help round up the other men.

Stetson was there then, talking rapidly to Bridger about what was happening. They had caught two of the men but the others were gone. Sophie didn't make out a whole lot of the other words, between his law enforcement lingo and her worry over Kai.

Crying in relief, she sagged against Bridger for a moment before hurrying over to get Kai where Hughes had looped her leash over something in his haste to get away. Kai lunged and whined at the end of her leash until she was free, and then she licked Sophie's face and whined some more.

Bridger moved closer to Poppy but told her to stay put. "We'll need to get a statement from you."

Sophie hoped they would also ask a lot of questions and find out whether or not the girl had been involved, though judging by the sheer terror on her face, Sophie would guess Poppy had either gotten in deeper than she had planned or she had been an unwilling participant in the plot to trap Sophie and Bridger.

"Your parents are sick with worry." Sophie hugged Kai, stroking her to comfort them both.

"Where are they?" Poppy had tears streaming down her face.

"Out looking for you. We'll let them know you're okay." Bridger gave her a stern look.

"They tried to warn me. Told me I was making the wrong sort of friends. But I felt so out of place with the popular kids at school and I just wanted friends." Poppy wiped at her eyes with the back of her hand.

"It's not too late to make changes in your life, Poppy." Sophie smiled at the girl.

"I know. I'm ready to try." Poppy tried for a wobbly grin in return. "Thank you."

Bridger was frowning, though. "Poppy, I need to ask you... Do you have any idea who the man wearing the mask was?"

Poppy shook her head. "No, I didn't see his face, either."

Bridger nodded but didn't give up. "Was there anything at all familiar about him, though? Did you recognize his voice or anything?"

Poppy cocked her head sideways and considered his question for a moment. "No. I really don't think so. I'm sorry."

Bridger thanked her for trying, but Sophie could see that something about the man's identity was troubling him.

She finally had the opportunity to ask him about it a

short while later while Poppy was giving her statement to the police. "The man in the mask…he was familiar somehow, wasn't he?"

Bridger turned to her, expression startled. "Yeah, he was. Did you think so, too?"

Sophie nodded. "I didn't really think so until you started asking Poppy about him. But the more I considered it, I realized he reminded me of someone in some way. But I can't quite put my finger on it. I don't think I know him."

"I know exactly what you're saying. I'm the same way. I don't know why he seems familiar." Bridger put his hands in his coat pockets. "But I find it especially strange that he was so protective of his identity."

Sophie agreed, but Bridger's brother Campbell approached before they could speak further. "I'm sorry, but there's no sign of your attackers. They must have jumped in their vehicles and headed for the hills."

"I'm sure." Bridger nodded. "Thanks for trying. I'd hoped you'd be here before they could get away. They had a lookout. Saw the lights and sirens too soon."

"Believe me, I wish we had come in without them, but we had to run hot to get here as fast as possible. I didn't realize you were in danger soon enough." Campbell shook his head, expression full of remorse.

"There was no way for you to know sooner. I'm just glad you got here when you did." Bridger clapped his brother on the back but then decided to hug him instead.

Poppy's parents arrived a few minutes later, hugging their daughter and crying. Before they left to take her home, they thanked Bridger, Sophie and Kai for all they had done to find her.

They talked a bit more about what had happened and what the men had looked like until the ambulances arrived.

"I wonder why the one guy kept his face covered the whole time?" Campbell was thinking aloud, but Bridger found it interesting that everyone wondered about that.

"I'm not sure, really. I guess there could be a lot of reasons, but none really make sense." He shook his head, but it didn't clear the thoughts that occupied his brain. He needed time to piece it all together.

"No, not if he was planning to kill you anyway. But maybe it will all make more sense once we catch up to him again."

Bridger admired his brother's confidence. He had thought they would catch him soon, as well, until tonight. Now he wasn't sure. He was simply weary and anxious to have Sophie and Kai safe.

SIXTEEN

The night had closed in on morning by the time they were able to return to the Cole ranch to get some sleep. Sophie slept fitfully throughout the early morning hours, however, and finally rose a little after seven thirty to find Bridger already returning from the barns while he spoke to someone on the phone. His expression was intense and he was soon scribbling some notes on a piece of paper, so she simply nodded at him and walked past to get a cup of coffee. She took it into the living room to give him privacy in the kitchen and found Caroline curled up watching videos on her phone.

After good-morning greetings, Caroline waved a hand toward the Christmas tree. "Mom's already gone off to do some last-minute shopping for the Christmas dinner she has planned. Will you still be here?"

Sophie sighed. "As much as I've enjoyed staying with your family, I'm afraid I need to get back home. My mother is alone. That's no way to spend the holiday."

"Why don't you bring her here?" Bridger's voice in the doorway surprised her. From the expression on his face, she thought maybe his offer had surprised him, too.

"Oh, we couldn't impose. Thank you for your generous offer, though." Sophie put a hand to her chest.

"It's really no imposition at all. At least think about it before you decide. Besides, if we don't catch this guy soon, it won't be safe for you to go home." Bridger raised one eyebrow at her.

"I had really hoped this all would be taken care of by now." Sophie grimaced.

"Me, too. Speaking of which, I just got some news. As soon as you're ready, we need to get moving. I thought you'd sleep longer, but since you didn't, we should take advantage of the time we have." Bridger turned to Caroline. "Can you feed the horses this evening if I'm not back?"

"Of course." Caroline's forehead creased in concern, however. "Be safe, though."

Sophie couldn't shake the feeling that Caroline had had something of a premonition about the way the day was going to turn out, and had to admit she had been feeling the same way since they'd gotten back to the ranch in the wee morning hours. She prayed silently for protection for them all. Whatever the day might bring, she sure hoped this would all be over soon.

Bridger didn't tell her what news he had received until she had changed clothes and she and Kai were loaded into the Jeep with him to leave the ranch. "The DEA has tracked down a name for Agent Benton's contact. I have an address and we're headed there now."

A shudder crept up Sophie's spine. "Did you recognize the name?"

Bridger craned his neck to double check behind him before backing out of the drive. "No, the man goes by the name of Roger Scully. Lives outside of Garland, looks like about fifteen minutes from here."

The house was a long way out of town, and even once

they reached the address, a lengthy driveway wound down and into a heavy stand of trees.

"Someone likes their privacy," Bridger commented.

The house and grounds were quiet, well maintained close to the house, but a sign warned of a security system as a fence came into view. It was a modest, ranch-style brick house with a small stoop entry.

As they got out, Sophie kept a tight grip on Kai's leash, unsure of what they might find.

"Stay behind me, just in case. And watch your back."

A quick knock brought the sound of shuffling feet toward the entry. When the door cracked open, a broad-shouldered man in his thirties peeked out at Sophie and Bridger, and from what she could see, a shotgun was in his hand. "Who is it?"

"Police. We just want to ask you a few questions." Bridger showed his badge. Kai stayed surprisingly calm at the end of her leash.

The man hesitated a moment, but with a soft curse, he opened the door wider to allow them in.

"Texas Ranger, huh? What's this about?" He eyed them both warily.

"Did you know a woman by the name of Sarah?" Bridger produced a photo of Agent Benton and as soon as the man got a good look, he sucked in a breath.

"I knew her by another name. But I know the face. Why do you ask?" He motioned for them to enter and sit down on the sofa in the living room.

Bridger thanked him but continued. "She's dead."

"What? Did they—" He suddenly stopped, leaving Bridger to wonder what he had been about to say. His face crumpled with pain.

"Mr. Scully, how did you know this woman?" Bridger softened his tone.

His eyes filled with tears that he thumbed away before trying again. "I think you'd better sit down."

The man leaned the shotgun against the wall. "She wasn't who you think she was."

Bridger nodded. "We know she was a federal agent. She was murdered in Garland the night the tornado hit. Someone tried to cover it up, but they did a really poor job. The storm must've hit before he could finish the job. We think the men she was investigating were on to her."

Sophie looked at Bridger, wondering how he knew this man was trustworthy. But he was right, for the man spoke up again then. "She left something with me. Said someone would come around looking for information if anything happened to her. I laughed at the time, told her she was being ridiculous. I guess she knew how close they were to finding her out, though. I should have protected her."

"What did she leave you, Mr. Scully?" Bridger prompted.

He frowned. "My real name's Dylan. Sullivan Dylan. You might as well know that, too. Sasha Benton was my sister."

"I'm so sorry." Bridger and Sophie both spoke at the same time.

Leaving the silence of shock in his wake, Sullivan rose to go into another room. When he returned, he was carrying a file. He handed it to Bridger and sat, tears rolling freely down his cheeks now.

They settled on the sofa and Sophie leaned into Bridger's shoulder as he opened the file. In it were photos, dozens of photos, and a sheaf of papers that looked like some kind of official report. At the top of the report was a name.

"Kelly Anderson? As in, the son of John Reilly Anderson?" Bridger stared up at Sullivan in disbelief.

Sophie sucked in a shocked breath. She immediately knew what had been so familiar about the guy in the mask. His voice, his demeanor, everything about him was reminiscent of his father. John Reilly Anderson was a senator. Kelly Anderson was the man she had seen in the hoodie the night of the fire, too. Skinny and high on something, he had still looked familiar, and now she knew why. What was a senator's son doing running a drug ring?

"Exactly him. I've been waiting on a contact from the DEA or news from Sasha. But now that I know she's gone, it's going to be up to us." Sullivan pulled something out of his pocket. A police badge. "I'm not a Texas Ranger or anything, but I'm trained in law enforcement."

Bridger nodded solemnly. "I think I know where we can find him. And I can have plenty of backup there in a matter of minutes."

Sullivan's face changed then, darkening and becoming stone-cold serious. He nodded.

"It's time. Let's go get him."

Bridger's thoughts were still reeling from finding out who the man was, but he made a few phone calls and soon had a team of men set up to be ready at a moment's notice. Now they had to get help from the inside.

He turned to Sophie. "I need you to get in touch with Poppy. Find out every hangout, house, pasture or whatever that she's ever been to with her friends from the Birch Street community center. I'll get someone checking on the warehouse to see what name is on it. It won't be Kelly Anderson's, but maybe we can learn what aliases he's using."

Sophie nodded. "What about the house where we thought

they were holding Poppy? The address where Agent Benton was found?"

"We're going to look into all of them." Bridger was tapping some notes into his phone screen.

"Not to brag, but I'm not bad with computer junk." This came from Sullivan.

"Perfect. That can save us some time." Bridger waited until the man retrieved a laptop and then began feeding him information.

Sophie had gone into another room to contact Poppy. By the time she returned with a list, it was only a matter of seconds before they had more names, along with all their addresses. Most of them had rap sheets, so they narrowed down the alias Anderson was using to a Bruce Hannibal.

"He owned the house where Agent Benton was found. He's our killer. The question is, what was she doing there?" Sophie groaned as if she should have known better.

"She was getting a confession." Sullivan spoke, but Bridger nodded in agreement.

"Wouldn't she have been wearing a wire?" Sophie asked.

"She likely was. A recording device, at least. That's what he was doing hanging out at the scene after the storm hit. He had to make sure he had gotten all the evidence. Only he didn't count on the file with the photos." Bridger gestured to the open file, a photo of Anderson coming out of the warehouse, head down and hood over his head staring at them from the top of the stack. Though his face had been partially shadowed by the hood, it was still obvious it was him.

"So we still need a confession?" Sophie looked horrified at the thought.

"Don't worry. We'll get it." Bridger wanted to reassure

her, but he knew she was right. This might be the hardest part of the case yet.

"What's the plan?" Sullivan braced his hands on his hips.

"We're going to this address. It's owned by one Rocky Lowry. He can answer some questions for us before we go for Anderson." Bridger pointed to the computer where Sullivan had compiled a spreadsheet of the data.

Taking the shortest route, they reached the house in just minutes. Sullivan followed at a safe distance behind them. But when they arrived at the address, it was a run-down clapboard house with little in the way of neighbors, reminiscent of the one where they had overheard the man talking on the phone the night before. Despite the barren winter season, it was obvious things had been allowed to sprout up significantly around the house and an outbuilding of some sort before the growing season was over. A decrepit-looking old ATV sat next to the outbuilding, though it was difficult to tell if the sheet metal structure was a shop or a barn. The scent of smoke from something stronger than a cigarette filtered through the vents of the Jeep and Sophie wrinkled her nose. There was a single vehicle in the driveway, an old white Ford truck. The house and grounds looked neglected and tired.

"Have we seen that truck before?" Sophie's brow wrinkled.

"It certainly seems familiar." Bridger eyed the ninety-something-model, half-ton pickup for a moment before it apparently clicked. "We saw it in town the night of the warehouse fire."

"That must be the reason. He was there." Sophie shuddered.

"I don't really like the looks of any of this." Bridger pulled into the drive behind the Ford. "Keep your guard up."

Sophie didn't miss the fact that he pulled his SIG before opening the driver's-side door. She reached for her door handle and paused. "Should I keep Kai on her leash?"

"I think so, for now. I don't know what we're about to find. Stay behind me." Bridger was already moving quietly toward the door.

When they reached the porch, however, the front door was slightly ajar, and on closer inspection, it looked like someone had forced entry. Bridger's brow furrowed beneath his cowboy hat.

"I don't like this at all." He knocked then gently eased open the door.

"Police. Anyone here?" He called the words loudly, but no answer came.

Bridger pushed the door open wider and Sophie followed, but she felt her eyes widen as he spoke again.

"Someone got here first."

Sophie swallowed hard as she saw what exactly Bridger referenced with his words. A man sat slumped over in a chair, a gunshot wound to his head just like the one Agent Benton had suffered. She recognized him as one of the men who had held Poppy in the warehouse. Bile rose up in her throat and Sophie looked away. Sullivan was coming in behind them.

"I guess we won't be talking to Mr. Lowry." His voice held more regret than surprise.

Kai whined then began to pull against her harness. "Bridger, I think someone's still here." Sophie whispered the words close to his ear.

Before they could react, however, a creak sounded on the porch behind them just before the door swung into Sophie, knocking Kai's leash from her hand as Sophie tumbled to the floor. She shrieked as rough hands grabbed for her, and the sound of more footsteps inside the house met her ears, the sound of a hammer click from a handgun chilling her blood in her veins even as Bridger and Sullivan both froze. Kai barked fiercely, trying to lunge at Sophie's attacker, but her attacker swung Sophie around in between himself and Kai.

"We meet again." The man with the deep voice hauled Sophie up hard against him. "This time we won't take so long to do away with you both. And that stupid dog, too."

Sophie's heart nearly stopped. They hadn't expected this.

Bridger had dropped his gun and had his hands in the air. Sullivan slowly did the same as three more men appeared from the back of the house, all waving guns at them threateningly.

"It's not too late to work out a deal." Bridger's voice was somehow calm, though Sophie wanted to scream in terror.

The harsh laugh in her ear sent a wave of revulsion through her. "A deal. That's cute. I don't want a deal. I can't be caught, you see. It would ruin everything. My future, my empire, my family… It's not possible. So, you see, I just have to kill you."

"Leaving a trail of bodies will only work so long. Eventually they will catch up with you." Bridger shook his head. He wasn't about to tell Anderson he already knew who he was. That would be a death sentence for all of them.

Sophie could feel the shrug the man gave him, though she couldn't see it. Surprisingly, her captor smelled like cologne and what she could see of his sleeve looked like a high-quality suit. How had she missed it before? He didn't fit in with the thugs he had surrounded himself with. He was a wealthy senator's son.

"It works for now. If it stops working, I'll try another way." The arrogance in the man's voice wasn't lost on Sophie. She didn't know whether his overabundance of confidence would work for or against them.

"You'll run out of time first." Bridger growled the words.

He laughed, his pitch a little maniacal. Was it the drugs? Sophie didn't know anything about it, other than hearsay. "I'll take my chances."

He jerked hard against Sophie's throat, causing Bridger to wince. She steeled her expression against the pain his harsh grip was causing. She didn't want to do anything to distract Bridger from getting them out of this safely.

"Meanwhile, we're going to take care of all the bodies at once. I really enjoyed the warehouse fire. I think I might like to try something like that again. That's what was planned for your little spy friend you found in the storm. But the weather didn't cooperate. If the storm had gotten here later, as it was supposed to, there wouldn't have been a body left to find. Only ashes." Anderson's voice was too nonchalant for his words. It somehow made him all the more repulsive. Sophie couldn't hold back the shudder.

"Are you saying you were going to burn the house around her after you shot her?" Bridger seized the opportunity, but Anderson didn't admit to anything, instead rambled on about that day.

"You know, sweetheart, I blame you and this beast of a dog. If you hadn't found the body so quickly, it would have disappeared and none of this would be happening right now. So, you see, you've brought this all on yourselves." He hissed the last.

"Why did you kill him?" Bridger jerked his chin toward Rocky Lowry. "I thought he was your right-hand man."

Anderson sighed. "He was, for a while. And a pretty

good one. But he knew too much. Started veering out of his lane, you know? Thought he was too important. That had to be remedied. People are lining up to be on my team these days."

"And the girl in the warehouse?" Bridger kept him talking. Surely, Campbell and Stetson would catch on if it took them long enough to hear from Bridger. He prayed they would, anyway.

"I don't really remember a girl in the warehouse." He paused. "Oh, yes. She started trying to tell us how to run the business. Wanted us to clean the machines better so people wouldn't die or something. We don't have time for that. I don't like when people interfere in my business."

Kai had been remarkably silent, though her hackles had been raised the whole time. Sullivan, too, had remained quiet, until now.

"We wouldn't want to slow down your production times. Did you know who she was?" Sullivan ground out the words.

"Who, the girl in the warehouse?" He was playing dumb, Sophie felt sure of it.

"The woman found in the storm debris." Sullivan's face was red and angry. He seemed to have had enough of this guy. She couldn't blame him for wanting justice.

"Oh. Yes, I do believe I found her out. It helps to know people in power. She was easily identified as a federal agent. One Sasha Benton, DEA. So, you see, now that you know I killed a federal agent, I simply must make sure you're all dead." He turned to one of his men. Hughes again, she thought.

"Tie them up. Make sure you take care of the dog, too."

Rough hands jerked Sophie to a wooden chair in the breakfast nook as the other men did the same to Bridger and Sullivan. Sophie couldn't hold in her gasps and grunts as the man handled her roughly, forcing her into the hard chair to tie her up. She struggled, though she knew it was futile. She wouldn't make it easy for him.

Kai whimpered and fought against the man holding her leash, but it did no good for any of them to fight. Kelly Anderson had the upper hand.

He lowered his gun to his side and walked over to stand in front of them then, obviously not finished with them just yet.

Before he could say whatever it was he had planned, however, a scrape at the roof came just before the door burst open wide and the windows filled with dark uniforms.

"Put your hands up, Anderson. You're surrounded."

Sophie almost sighed in relief, until she realized they weren't saved yet.

Anderson raised his gun and began to fire at the open door. The other men began to scatter, trying to find any exit away from the team of officers outside. "Torch it!" He screamed the words into the chaos.

Kai began whining again, causing Hughes to yell and continue to jerk on her leash. It made Sophie angry.

Lord, help us all get out of here safely, she silently prayed.

She realized as the men continued to scatter and yell in the chaos that Hughes had tied Kai to her chair and had started pouring some sort of liquid around them. Accelerant of some kind, she feared. Then he dropped a match and ran for it.

Kai started out whining, but as the flames jumped higher, she began to bark. Fear for her filled Sophie. It broke Sophie's heart to think of Kai suffering because of her own actions. It renewed her strength to know that Kai was depending on her, also. She rocked and swayed, trying to get her chair to tip or move so she could pull Kai farther from the flames. She managed to scoot backward a bit, but the flames continued to lick closer as well.

Bridger, also, was trying to work free. Sophie fervently hoped he could break loose. The men had been in a hurry, which worked in Sophie and Bridger's favor because they hadn't tied them as tightly as they might've otherwise. Sophie mimicked Bridger's efforts as she realized that, pulling and jerking at her hands as hard as she could in an attempt to break free. The result was a great deal of pain in her wrists, but nothing like the smoke and flames would soon cause her lungs if they didn't get out.

Coughing, she paused long enough to scrape her chair a bit farther back to give Kai a little more room. She ran around to the inside of Sophie's chair away from the flames at Sophie's encouragement.

She could hear the sounds of the officers outside, yelling and firing their weapons as they rounded up the men bent on escape. It was comforting to know they were going to be brought to justice, but Sophie sure wished they would hurry and come rescue them. As it was, things were still up to Bridger, Sophie and Sullivan.

And Kai was her responsibility. "Come on, girl. It's okay. Stay back as far as you can. I'm trying to get us loose." Sophie talked to her the whole while, calming herself as much as Kai in the process. The smoke made it more difficult to see Bridger, but she could still hear him making efforts to get himself loose.

Sullivan also scooted and scraped, trying to dislodge his own ties. He was farther away, but she could still sense his own urgency.

The sirens were closer now, but the flames were higher,

too, and Sophie feared the men might have left behind other explosive materials. She was sweating in her heavy winter clothing as the flames scorched the air around them. With a mighty heave, she thrust her shoulders out and wrists apart. A small give in the ties was the result, so she repeated the action again and again. It loosened a tiny fraction more each time.

She was just about free when Bridger exclaimed in victory. "I'm loose!"

"I'm almost there. Get Kai out. Please!" She shouted above the roar of the fire.

"I'm getting you both out. Sullivan is already free of his ties." Bridger coughed, but he was there, finishing off the knots at her wrists to free her.

Sophie jumped up, making quick work of Kai's leash where it was tied to her chair while Bridger checked the smoke-filled air to be sure Sullivan was heading for the exit.

Sophie gave Kai the order to get out and she bolted through the flames, now free of her leash, fully expecting Sophie and Bridger to follow. Sullivan was right behind Kai when Bridger gave him the order to go. Sophie stumbled, however, as she was trying to leap through a gap in the flames encircling them. She went to her knees with a gasp, but it only made her cough harder. The fire crackled and sizzled around her and she felt a lightheadedness from the dissipating oxygen as the flames greedily consumed it. She tried to get to her feet, but her body refused to cooperate.

"Bridger!" she called weakly. She couldn't see him, but she knew he was close. He had just been right there beside her.

She tried to pull her jacket over her sweating nose and mouth to block out the suffocating smoke, but the heat, her exhaustion and the lack of sufficient oxygen combined to make every move she made exponentially more difficult. Her body was wracked with coughs again, but then she felt her body go limp as her limbs refused to cooperate with the screaming of her mind to get out.

Everything began to fade to black just as she felt strong arms come up around her, lifting her away from the ground, but all she could do was give in to the darkness.

SEVENTEEN

Bridger gently laid Sophie on the ground far from the inferno as the uniformed officers flooded the area rounding up the escaped men. A blast shook the ground only seconds after they were clear. Anderson had been shot multiple times by the team as he had tried to flee and though he hadn't heard for sure yet, Bridger doubted he was still alive. But Bridger's sole concern at the moment was Sophie.

Kai whined, trotted around her master and back, and licked Sophie's face unceasingly in an insistent little dance until at last Sophie's eyes fluttered open.

"What—" A cough cut off her question. She tried to sit up but Bridger eased her back down.

"Easy. Take it easy. An ambulance is on the way." Bridger stroked her hair away from her sweat-slicked cheeks and forehead. He inhaled, silently breathing back out a prayer of thanks.

"Kai." Sophie said the dog's name on a sigh of relief. She didn't say more, just laid a hand on her canine as Kai whined and laid her head on Sophie's chest. Sophie closed her eyes again.

"She's fine. We're all going to be fine." But Bridger coughed again as well. He hadn't been much better off than Sophie when they made it out, falling to his knees twice before getting her far away from the building. Sullivan had made it out just behind Kai, but he had stumbled to the ground in exhaustion as soon as he was clear of the flaming structure, and if Bridger wasn't mistaken, he had sustained a pretty good burn to one arm.

"Ambulance is almost here." Campbell appeared at his elbow. Bridger had shucked his coat, but now the cold air rapidly cooled the sweat that covered him beneath his shirt and jeans, making him shiver in response.

An officer was seeing to Sullivan's injuries a few yards away until responders could take over. Bridger felt a pang of sorrow for the man at the loss of his sister. Now that this was over, it would sink in fast.

The ambulance stopped behind one of the pumper trucks the firefighters had just arrived in. They had the blaze nearly out and white smoke roiled in the night sky above.

Campbell waved a medic in their direction as the men and women began to get out of the trucks, sirens off but lights still flaring brightly.

Sophie's collapse had made him consider things from a new angle. He had spent all this time trying to convince himself to keep her at arm's length so he wouldn't get hurt when they inevitably had to go their separate ways. But he had realized when she'd gone down that it was too late for that. He had been scared for her, and not just a little. Terrified, even, to think that something might happen to her. It was too late to keep himself from falling in love with her. He had already fallen for her.

So now, he wondered why he would consider living without her, no matter how much time either of them might or might not have left. He wanted to spend whatever time they had with Sophie. He couldn't imagine his life any longer without her in it.

The paramedics and EMTs swarmed on them then, one moving toward Sophie and another intent on giving Bridger some oxygen as well. The woman looked him over for other injuries first, giving her partner a nod when she had finished. The paramedic jerked his head toward the truck they had driven in. "Come with me, sir. Let's get you back up to snuff."

Bridger could barely see Sophie from where he sat receiving oxygen in the back of one of the ambulances, but he kept an eye on her as best he could. He didn't know how he would be able to let her out of his sight after tonight. She kept Kai close while the team attended to her, but the dog seemed to be no worse for wear after escaping the fire.

Campbell approached a few minutes later. "Good news. We think we got all of them."

Bridger exhaled in relief. "Including Kelly Anderson?" He had to be sure.

"Anderson has someone bigger to answer to now. He's dead. If the bullets didn't finish him, the blast did. He was still close enough to sustain some burns when it blew. I suspect there will be a lot of press about it. Better brace yourself for that." Campbell winced slightly. He hated the press almost as much as Bridger did. The Cole family definitely wasn't in law enforcement because of any desire to be in the spotlight.

"Sophie seems to be okay. She didn't sustain any lasting injuries?" Bridger was watching her again, and Campbell followed his gaze.

"She's fine. Really. But I suspect you're going to have to see for yourself." He chuckled. He clapped his brother on the shoulder gently before moving along to check on Sullivan. They would want statements from them all.

News reporters began to arrive on the scene, but, thankfully, Campbell and some of the other officers handled it and kept them from questioning Sophie, Sullivan or Bridger. Kai was curled up at Sophie's feet when Bridger was finally released to go to her.

"You're okay?" Bridger looked her over thoroughly, afraid he might have missed something.

"Thanks to you." She smiled sweetly at him. Kai raised her head to give him an adoring look as well. He gave her furry head a good rub before focusing on Sophie again.

"You're safe. Anderson is dead. They've rounded up the others and they'll all be going to prison for a good long time." Bridger clasped her hand and realized it was cold. He rubbed it between his hands to warm it.

"I hate it for his family. I wish there could have been another way. But I can't say I'm not relieved to know he won't be coming after me anymore." Sophie's face reflected her compassionate response.

At that moment, a petite figure approached, and at first, Bridger didn't recognize her. Lydia had scrubbed her face clean, and her dark hair was loose, falling in gentle waves over her shoulder. She was dressed in a soft pink sweater and blue jeans with a tan jacket over both. She looked young and vulnerable.

"Can I talk to you guys for a minute?" Lydia's voice had lost some of the hard edge it had held before.

"Of course." Sophie responded first, but she glanced at Bridger. He was nodding.

"First off, I wanted to apologize for misleading you. We were...coerced, to put it nicely. But now that it's safe, I want you to know, I'm going back home to live with my parents. I have a friend there who offered to help me get a job and I plan to go back to school part time. It won't be easy, but I think over time I can repair my relationship with my parents." Lydia ducked her head.

"That's wonderful news." Sophie beamed at the young woman.

"I wish you all the best of luck, Lydia." Bridger offered his hand.

Lydia grasped it reluctantly. "I also wanted to say thank you. To you both. If it weren't for you, I wouldn't be getting this second chance. Is it true Sarah was actually an FBI agent?"

"She was with the Drug Enforcement Agency. Her real name was Sasha Benton. I hope she can receive a proper memorial service now that her undercover case has been wrapped up." Bridger explained it to the girl gently. "I appreciate that you and your friends had a memorial for her, though."

Lydia blushed. "It wasn't much of one for someone of her stature. And, honestly, those people aren't a part of my life anymore. Unless they get clean, I can't be around them. I won't chance it."

Bridger simply nodded. "I understand that."

"You'll make new friends easily." Sophie smiled and grasped Lydia's hand.

"I'm going to go back to my natural color, too." Lydia fingered a strand of her hair, cheeks flushing a little more.

"I'm sure it's beautiful no matter what color it is." Sophie gave her a nod of reassurance.

"This just isn't really me. I let others talk me into it. Will you let me know about Sarah's—um, Agent Benton's—memorial service?" Lydia slipped a piece of paper from the pocket of her loose jeans. "This is the number to reach my mom."

"Of course. I'll be sure to let you know. And, Lydia? Merry Christmas." Sophie hugged her.

"Thank you. And Merry Christmas to both of you as well." Lydia smiled and turned to go. Then she turned back. "You're going to be okay, right?"

Sophie nodded. "I'll be just fine. And Kai, too. Thank you."

Lydia drifted away then, almost silently.

"I'm glad she's going back home. I sure hope everything works out for her." Sophie fixed her big hazel eyes on Bridger and he almost forgot what she was saying.

He took a deep breath. "Me, too. She seems genuinely sorry."

"I'm sure everything she's seen lately has had a pretty profound effect on her." Sophie shook her head sorrowfully.

Bridger nodded, but after a pause, he spoke again.

"As soon as you're released, I want to get going. I don't know how long Campbell and the others can hold off the press." He jerked his head toward a news van.

"She's free to go in less than five minutes." A paramedic spoke from somewhere near Bridger's elbow.

When he disappeared again, Bridger confessed, "I was so afraid I'd lost you."

He folded her gently in his arms and she melted into him. After a few seconds like this, he found he wanted nothing more than to kiss her.

"Sophie…"

But before he could ask her permission, she kissed him first, her soft lips meeting his in a gentle expression of love and wonder. He drew her closer and deepened the kiss until a throat cleared behind him.

"Sorry to interrupt, but I thought you might like to know she's free to go now." The paramedic had a hint of amusement in his voice, and when Bridger turned to thank him, there was definitely a twinkle in his eye.

It seemed hours before they finally got back to the ranch. Bridger had expected the house to be dark thanks to the lateness of the hour, but several windows glowed in anticipation of their arrival.

"Thank goodness you're all safe." Dana Cole wrapped each of them in a hug in turn, even Kai. She motioned for them all to get up the stairs. "I have some homemade chicken soup, if you want to eat something after you shower. If you'd rather go on to bed, I fully understand."

Bridger wanted to sleep, in his mind, but his body told him it would be a while before he could relax into the exhaustion that consumed him enough to rest. "That sounds great, actually. I doubt I can sleep."

Sophie nodded as well. "It's ridiculous, as tired as I am, but I don't think I can, either, just yet."

"Sure. I'll get some bowls ready." Dana shooed each of them on to the shower.

Campbell had gone back to finish up reports after they'd left, since his shift wouldn't be over for a while yet. Kai, just relieved to be somewhere safe, curled up in the corner and promptly went to sleep while Bridger's mother quietly puttered around the kitchen as if it wasn't the middle of the night.

The quiet house was a comfort to Bridger. But he couldn't help thinking of how afraid he had been for Sophie as his thoughts began to settle. She had come to mean so much to him in such a short period of time. As he settled at the table in the kitchen, his mother seemed to read his thoughts.

"You can relax, Bridger. Sophie's going to be fine." She

smiled at him with the knowing expression only a mother could get away with.

"What?"

He knew the one-word question sounded silly and juvenile, but he didn't have a clue how to respond at the moment.

"You know what. I can see it every time you look at her. She's special." She settled into the chair across from him and waited until he met her eyes.

"She is, but… I don't know if she's ready to love again." Bridger told her then about Sophie's previous marriage.

"Why don't you let Sophie decide?" She gave him a gentle pat on the shoulder as she rose from her seat.

Footsteps sounded on the stairs and soon Sophie appeared, gratefully accepting her bowl of soup. Her hair was damp and she had scrubbed her face clean of any makeup. Bridger thought she had never looked more beautiful.

"If you don't mind, I'm going to retire for the rest of the evening." Dana gave them both a knowing look. "I'll see you both in the morning. Oh…and, Sophie, we would love for you to invite your mother here for Christmas. Just think it over."

When she was gone, Bridger grinned at her. "As I said, your mother is welcome here for Christmas. My mom loves a big crowd. We've already invited Sullivan and Mr. Brownley, though who knows if he'll come."

Sophie smiled. "I'd honestly love to, if you're sure."

But then her expression darkened and she dropped her gaze. "Bridger, I know we were both caught up in our emotions tonight. If you didn't—"

She stopped, and Bridger's stomach clenched. He should have been more open with her.

"Sophie, look at me." When she did, he spoke the words

that had been burning inside him all night long. For days, honestly.

"I love you. I want nothing more than to keep you in my life from now on."

Her eyes widened and then she smiled a wide, beautiful smile that lit up her entire face, "I love you, too. And I want that as well."

He rose and walked to where she sat, pulled her up into his arms, and kissed her again in the warmth of the kitchen, putting all the feelings he had been holding back into his kiss.

EIGHTEEN

Sophie had never experienced Christmas like this.

The Cole family could only be described as jolly as they gathered around the beautifully decorated table, the scents of roast turkey and ham, yeast rolls, pies and all the trimmings mingling in the air. In addition to the other Christmas decorations, the dining room table had been adorned with lit red tapers amid circles of flocked garland and pinecones, each place set with fine white Christmas china. The soft notes of instrumental Christmas carols filled the air and contentment such as Sophie had rarely felt filled her to bursting.

Georgia had indeed come to the ranch with Sophie for Christmas, and Sullivan had accepted the invitation, also, arriving in time to enjoy a good long chat with Campbell and Stetson as they waited for the meal to be settled on the table. Caroline bustled around the kitchen, having requested to learn how to "do Christmas dinner" from her mother, and Dana had joyfully obliged.

Dana cleared her throat and thanked everyone for being there as a hush fell over the gathering. She asked Bridger if he would bless the food so they could begin.

They had just settled at the long dining table set with

dishes rimmed with sprigs of holly and begun to pass the serving dishes when the doorbell rang.

"I'll get it." Bridger rose from his place beside Sophie and went to the door, returning a few minutes later behind Mr. Brownley, who ducked his head before speaking.

"I'm sorry I'm late. I almost decided against accepting your hospitality but... Well, I really wanted to come, you see." His face turned red at the admission. But then his eyes fixed on Sullivan, widening in surprise.

"Sully? Is that you?" Mr. Brownley scuttled closer to him. "My eyesight's not what it used to be, so forgive me, but—"

"Uncle Richard?" Sullivan rose and clasped the man in a hearty embrace. "I thought you'd moved away."

The elderly man's eyes watered. "Away from town is all. I admit, I let everyone believe I went farther. I didn't want to be a burden anymore."

"Uncle Richard, no one saw you as a burden. Come. Sit here and enjoy this meal with us, and later you and I have some catching up to do." Sullivan urged the elderly man to a chair beside his own.

Sophie felt tears gathering at the corners of her eyes as she watched the two men reconnecting, and she said a little silent prayer of thanks as Bridger returned to his chair and squeezed her hand. She had thought of Mr. Brownley often since their encounter, and admittedly had worried about the elderly man living alone. Knowing he had family to help look after him warmed her heart and eased her mind.

Dana and Georgia chatted comfortably across the table, as Sophie had imagined they would, and Kai and the corgis curled by the fire, looking up occasionally in hopes that they might receive a small amount of scraps when the meal was done. Caroline, Stetson and Campbell had all hugged

Sophie when she and her mother had arrived, Caroline whispering in her ear about how glad she was that Sophie was back. She joked about being outnumbered by the men, but Sophie felt there was a little truth in Caroline's desire for another ally.

The meal passed quickly with all the joviality and delicious food, but when they were finally alone for a few minutes after everyone had finished, Bridger pulled Sophie in close.

"Can we make this official?" He whispered the words close to her ear, causing a tingle of warmth to swirl through her.

"What do you mean?" Her breath caught.

"Can I call you my girlfriend?" He pulled back and grinned at her with a twinkle in his eyes.

"Of course!" Sophie snuggled into his chest. She forced down the pang of regret that he hadn't asked her to be something a little more permanent, like his fiancée, but she realized it was a little bit soon for that.

But she was ready.

Sophie had spoken to her supervisor at the historic society where she worked and while she would have to drive to the local historic sites occasionally for work, there had been a position available that would allow her to work remotely the majority of the time, meaning it wouldn't matter if she moved to Oak Ridge, which she had admittedly considered. She just hadn't found the perfect place yet. No, the truth was she would never find a better place than the Cole ranch, but she needed a place of her own. At least, it seemed so for now.

"Good." Bridger's deep voice rumbled against her ear where she was pressed close. "Because I have other plans. But I should probably convince you one step at a time."

Her heart leapt in response to his words. Could he possibly be thinking the same thing she was? Did he want to marry her? Sophie told herself to be reasonable. After all, they had only known each other a short time. It would be wise to get to know one another better first.

"You can be very persuasive." Sophie tried to keep the teasing note from her voice, but it was there. His smile widened in response.

"I hope so. Because I have a lot to persuade you of in the future." His teasing tone sent her insides into a little flutter of a happy dance. She was definitely in love with this man. She decided to tell him so.

"I love you, Bridger Cole." She felt her cheeks heat at the way his eyes widened. Was she being too bold?

But all doubts fled when he spoke. "I love you, Sophie."

Bridger pulled back and grinned at her before kissing her long and slow.

Bridger could barely contain his own enthusiasm. If he wasn't mistaken, Sophie was just as anxious to share their lives together as he was. But in all the excitement of finding Agent Benton's killer, he had forgotten it had only been a couple of short weeks since they had met. He felt like he knew Sophie so well already. But common sense told him he needed to give them a little more time before jumping into things.

Watching her interact with his family today had convinced him, though, that this was where Sophie belonged. He knew, also, that she would be concerned about her mother living so far away, but he thought he had a solution to that as well.

There was a small house with a few acres just down the road, on a property that adjoined the ranch. It had been vacant for a few months, but the owners hadn't yet decided whether or not to sell. Just yesterday, he had heard from a Realtor friend that the couple had decided to put it on the market. He had called Bridger first, since the acreage adjoined his ranch. Bridger had, of course, jumped at the opportunity to purchase it. He'd checked out the house and found it was in very good condition. He planned to offer it to Sophie and Georgia to rent if they were interested.

He was more than ready to have Sophie nearby after she had been gone the past couple of days. He honestly couldn't get the papers signed fast enough.

"Hey, Sophie. I have some news I need to share with you." Bridger watched as her eyes widened.

"What's that?" Sophie slid her hand under his arm.

"I recently learned about a real estate opportunity." He told her about the house, how it joined his property and that he had decided to buy. "The thing is, I'm going to need some renters. It's a small house, very affordable, but neat and cute."

He paused for a moment, watching her emotions play across her face. "None of your siblings are ready to move out?"

Her words were cautious, as if she wasn't sure what he was getting at.

He decided to alleviate her concerns. "I was actually thinking I'd love it if you were close by. There's plenty of room for you and your mother. Do you think she would mind moving here? It's in good shape and it's a nice place, even though it's on the small side." Bridger gave her a pleading look.

It turned out to be unnecessary. "Oh, Bridger! We would love that. I mean if we could afford it. But it would be wonderful to live so close."

He grinned broadly. "I imagine we can work out something affordable on the rent. You don't mind leaving your home?"

"To be honest, not at all. I rented the cheapest thing I could find once I got a decent job, and it's never really been my favorite." She wrinkled her nose. "Can we see the house?"

"How about tomorrow? I'm trying to get the Realtor to rush things so I can get the papers signed. He can let us in." Bridger pulled her close.

"Tomorrow would be great! I'll see if Mom is okay with it." Sophie leaned in and kissed him, this time on the cheek. "You're so amazing, Bridger Cole."

The next day, Bridger took Sophie and Georgia to the property. Georgia was immediately enamored with the place, and Sophie, too, found the quaint little house adorable and inviting. It sat off the road just enough to be somewhat hidden in the trees like a little fairy-tale cottage, and the inside was cozy and well designed. The walls were freshly painted in a neutral taupe and the floors were a mix of hardwood and plush carpet throughout. There were several windows letting in natural light, a small front porch and a perfect-sized patio at the back looking out onto the prairie. The house seemed to be no more than ten or fifteen years old, but the bathrooms had been updated as well as the kitchen, its beautiful, sunny breakfast nook facing the sunrise in the east and lined with cheerful white cabinets.

It was charming and lovely.

"I can't think of anything more perfect!" Georgia gushed. "Are you sure you want to rent it?"

Bridger pulled Sophie into his arms. "Having Sophie this close would mean more to me than you can imagine."

"Well, then." Georgia cleared her throat and sent Sophie a knowing look. "How soon can we move in?"

EPILOGUE

Bridger waited for Sophie on the front porch, nerves jolting through him. It was mild for the thirty-first of December, but he didn't notice the temperature at all. When her Jeep came up the drive, excitement swept through him.

He had some serious things to discuss with her.

Bridger had planned to wait a little longer, but since Christmas, all he had wanted to do was spend time with Sophie, and unless he was mistaken, she felt the same way.

Sophie stepped out of the Jeep, looking adorable in a gray sweater and blue jeans, a sturdy pair of low-heeled boots beneath. He was glad, for they might have some walking to do. She let Kai out of the back seat, and the dog ran some big circles around the yard before running up to greet Bridger. Then she ran to the door, excited to see the rest of the family and her corgi friends. It had become a routine over the past week.

After a sweet kiss of greeting, Bridger took Sophie's hand. "How do you feel about taking a little walk with me before it gets dark?"

Sophie shrugged, questions in her eyes. "I don't have any objections to that."

Bridger took her around the barn and through a handful of horses gathered in one of the pens. Opening a gate, they walked out through a pasture full of shiny, plump Black Angus cattle and kept walking.

"Where are we going?" Sophie finally asked.

"Right up here. I want to show you something." Bridger led her to a slight rise that had a pretty view of the pastures all around them.

"Wow, this is lovely," Sophie said as they slowed.

"I'm thinking it would make a perfect place to build a house." Bridger stopped.

She turned to look at him, and he dropped to one knee. "Oh."

It was a soft gasp, but he continued, not waiting for her to say more.

"I think it would be a perfect place to raise our children. That is, if you'll agree to be my wife." He pulled a stunning oval diamond from his pocket and held it up to her. "I love you, Sophie. Marry me?"

"Seriously?" She put both hands to her face.

"Nothing would make me happier than to have you become my wife." Bridger grinned.

"Oh, yes! Yes, a thousand times."

He slid the ring on her finger and rose to kiss her.

From out of nowhere, Kai came zooming in, making loops around their legs as they embraced.

"Where did you even come from, girl? You were in the house." Bridger laughed.

Sophie's laughter echoed all around them. "Kai didn't want to be left out."

"Never." Bridger reassured her, bending to scratch Kai behind the ears. She panted and smiled up at them.

"She seems to approve," Sophie said.

"Good." Bridger straightened and kissed her again. "Because I can't wait to make you my wife."

As she wholeheartedly agreed, he pulled her to him and she sighed into his embrace. "How soon can we wed?"

He laughed and she kissed him this time, wrapping both arms around the man she loved. "As soon as possible."

* * * * *

*If you liked this story from Sommer Smith,
check out her previous Love Inspired Suspense books.*

Under Suspicion
Attempted Abduction
Ranch Under Siege
Wyoming Cold Case Secrets
Wyoming Ranch Ambush
Deadly Treasure Hunt
Deadly Ranch Abduction

Available now from Love Inspired Suspense!

Find more great reads at www.LoveInspired.com.

Dear Reader,

Thank you for joining Bridger, Sophie and Kai on their journey to find justice. I was inspired to write Kai by my daughter's Bernese Mountain dog, Bella, and her sweet, loving nature. Her ancestors have worked as farm dogs because of their herding abilities, but they also sometimes assist as search and rescue dogs since they work so well with people. Additionally, they make great therapy dogs in modern times because of their gentle nature.

I hope you enjoyed the story, and if you'd like to contact me, you can find me on Facebook as Sommer N. Smith, Author, or email me at sommersmithauthor@gmail.com.

Blessings,
Sommer

Get up to 4 Free Books!

We'll send you 2 free books from each series you try PLUS a free Mystery Gift

FREE Value Over $25

Both the **Love Inspired®** and **Love Inspired® Suspense** series feature compelling novels filled with inspirational romance, faith, forgiveness and hope.

YES! Please send me 2 FREE novels from the Love Inspired or Love Inspired Suspense series and my FREE gift (gift is worth about $10 retail). After receiving them, if I don't wish to receive any more books, I can return the shipping statement marked "cancel." If I don't cancel, I will receive 6 brand-new Love Inspired Larger-Print books or Love Inspired Suspense Larger-Print books every month and be billed just $7.19 each in the U.S. or $7.99 each in Canada. That is a savings of 20% off the cover price. It's quite a bargain! Shipping and handling is just 50¢ per book in the U.S. and $1.25 per book in Canada.* I understand that accepting the 2 free books and gift places me under no obligation to buy anything. I can always return a shipment and cancel at any time by calling the number below. The free books and gift are mine to keep no matter what I decide.

Choose one:
☐ **Love Inspired Larger-Print** (122/322 BPA G36Y)
☐ **Love Inspired Suspense Larger-Print** (107/307 BPA G36Y)
☐ **Or Try Both!** (122/322 & 107/307 BPA G36Z)

Name (please print)

Address   Apt. #

City   State/Province   Zip/Postal Code

Email: Please check this box ☐ if you would like to receive newsletters and promotional emails from Harlequin Enterprises ULC and its affiliates. You can unsubscribe anytime.

Mail to the Harlequin Reader Service:
IN U.S.A.: P.O. Box 1341, Buffalo, NY 14240-8531
IN CANADA: P.O. Box 603, Fort Erie, Ontario L2A 5X3

Want to explore our other series or interested in ebooks? **Visit www.ReaderService.com or call 1-800-873-8635.**

---

*Terms and prices subject to change without notice. Prices do not include sales taxes, which will be charged (if applicable) based on your state or country of residence. Canadian residents will be charged applicable taxes. Offer not valid in Quebec. This offer is limited to one order per household. Books received may not be as shown. Not valid for current subscribers to the Love Inspired or Love Inspired Suspense series. All orders subject to approval. Credit or debit balances in a customer's account(s) may be offset by any other outstanding balance owed by or to the customer. Please allow 4 to 6 weeks for delivery. Offer available while quantities last.

Your Privacy—Your information is being collected by Harlequin Enterprises ULC, operating as Harlequin Reader Service. For a complete summary of the information we collect, how we use this information and to whom it is disclosed, please visit our privacy notice located at https://corporate.harlequin.com/privacy-notice. Notice to California Residents – Under California law, you have specific rights to control and access your data. For more information on these rights and how to exercise them, visit https://corporate.harlequin.com/california-privacy. For additional information for residents of other U.S. states that provide their residents with certain rights with respect to personal data, visit https://corporate.harlequin.com/other-state-residents-privacy-rights/.